When A Savage Falls For A Good Girl 2:

A Crazy Hood Love

Tina J

1

Copyright 2020

Warning:

This book is strictly Urban Fiction and the story is **NOT**

REAL!

Characters will not behave the way you want them to; nor will

they react to situations the way you think they should. Some of

them may be drug addicts, kingpins, savages, thugs, rich, poor,

ho's, sluts, haters, bitter ex-girlfriends or boyfriends, people

from the past and the list can go on and on. That is what Urban

Fiction mostly consists of. If this isn't anything you foresee

yourself interested in, then do yourself a favor and don't read it

because it's only going to piss you off. ☺☺

Also, the book will not end the way you want so please be

advised that the outcome will be based solely on my own

thoughts and ideas. Thanks so much to my readers, supporters,

publisher and fellow authors and authoress for the support.

Author Tina J

Previously…

"Thanks Mr. Kruz, I had a good time in Mexico." Rhythm's son said when we got off the plane.

The day I fucked up at the doctor's office with Zahra, I picked up Rhythm and her son and went to Mexico. I needed a vacation and since we've become so close I didn't wanna go without her.

At first, she told me no and I had done enough for her with the shopping sprees. But once I told her the tickets were already paid for, she broke and came. The funny thing is, I owned a jet and we left from a private airport. I brought Kash with us so her son wouldn't he bored. Her and my brother hit it off good too. He did ask if she or Kalila had any little sisters. *Nasty motherfucker.*

I had to tell Kash he better not teach him how to steal and if he did while we were out there, I was gonna feed him to the sharks. Jamaica and Kalila came to chill on the third day and we had a ball.

4

During our time there, we toured a bunch of different spots, took Axel and Kash to different water parks and of course shopping. Rhythm didn't have a lot of money but she did pay for dinner every night and I appreciated it. The little things meant a lot more to a nigga than trying to impress me with other stuff.

The last night in Mexico, Rhythm and I had the freakiest sex ever. Nothing is off limits as it is, but we were outside on the beach doing anything to one another. When we finished, she confessed falling in love with me. She also admitted, it's probably because she's been single for so long it wasn't hard. I told her in these last six months, I felt the same because I did.

Rhythm is like a breath of fresh air for me. She's a great mother to her son and her loyalty to Kalila and her mom is commendable, which is why Jamaica and I furnished the entire upstairs of their newly renovated house. Well, we gave them the money because I damn sure don't have time to shop.

"Anytime, lil man." All four of us got in the truck and I drove to drop Kash off first. I offered for her to come in and she gave me the finger.

"Ma, can you drop me off at the hospital and take the truck?" I hopped in and sped off. My father said, my mother just left because Zahra was about to deliver. I was both excited and disappointed because I hated who my child's mother is gonna be.

"Yea, is everything ok?"

"Zahra's in labor."

"Really! Are you excited?" She had a smile on her face. I thought she'd be upset but I guess being on your grown woman shit, won't allow it.

"Yes and no." I pulled off in route to the hospital.

"Yes, because she's my daughter and no, due to who mother is."

"Well, you picked her." We both laughed.

I parked in front of the hospital, and waited for her to get in the driver's seat. We kissed, I watched her pull off and ran in to ask where the labor and delivery floor is. Once she told me, I couldn't get there fast enough.

"Is she here yet?" I asked my mother who was coming out the room.

"Not yet. They're prepping her and the doctor said she isn't fully dilated yet."

"Oh." I went over to the chairs and sat down.

"You're not going in?"

"For what?"

"To see your daughter being born." I leaned back in the chair and stared at her. How could a woman support another doing dumb shit is beyond me?

"Honestly, I'm not sure if the kid is mine." We may have taken the test and they confirmed it, however; after Zahra sucked my dick, I was convinced she had been with that nigga for much longer than she said. There's no way in hell she gave him head once and did it with no problem. She's a nurse too, which means she could've had the results changed.

"Kruz why are you treating her like this? Four years is a long time to flush the relationship down the drain." I hopped

7

up and got in her face. My phone started vibrating but whoever it is had to wait. I needed to say this shit and make sure she heard me.

"I didn't make shit go down the drain. She did when she started spending time with someone else. You seem to forget that I'm the one you birthed and not her."

"Son. I'm..."

"I'm over the bullshit with you and her. We aren't ever getting back together and when you see me with Rhythm, you better not disrespect or challenge her."

"She's your woman now?"

"Yup and you or Zahra ain't changing it." I snatched the phone off my hip and answered, still looking at her.

"Hello." Rhythm was distraught and I could barely understand her.

"Babe, I don't mean to call at a time like this but she fucked up everything. My entire room is destroyed and..."

"Hold on. Who did what?" I told her to calm down and speak slow.

"I came home after dropping you off and went to give Axel a bath. Kruz, everything you brought is thrown out in the backyard. She either took a knife or scissors to my bed, sheets and rug. I know it's Zahra because her car is parked in front of the house and it wasn't a break in."

"I'ma handle it."

"Kruz, my son is asking who would do this to my room. I can't tell him she did it because he loves her."

"Babe, I got you. Relax and I'll be there after she delivers." I hung up and put the phone on my hip.

"You're going to her while Zahra's in labor?" I stopped and turned around.

"I'd quit while I was ahead or you're gonna regret it." She saw my face and put her hands up in surrender.

I stormed in the room, yanked this dumb bitch up by the hair and made her look at me. I could hear the machine beeping fast and her holding her stomach and gave zero fucks. What she did is unacceptable and she's about to hear my mouth.

9

"What you did was childish as fuck and I'm gonna make sure you're dealt with after having this baby."

"Kruz please stop." Her hands were tryna pry mine off.

"Shut the fuck up bitch. You're lucky this is all I'm doing." I slammed her head in the pillow and turned to see her mother walking in.

WHAP! She smacked fire from Zahra.

"How dare you come in my house and destroy her room like that?" I stared down at the pictures Rhythm sent and got mad all over again.

"Ma, she don't deserve him."

"Oh, and a woman who's been opening her legs to God knows who during a relationship does?" Zahra put her head down.

"I raised you better than this and I pray my granddaughter doesn't grow up doing the same." She cursed Zahra out after each contraction and I didn't feel bad. My mother stood there watching and I dared her to say a word.

After ten hours of being in labor, my daughter finally graced us with her presence. She weighed seven pounds and 6 ounces. My mom said she looks just like me but she would say that being she's team Zahra. I ended up calling my pops up and asked him to come get her. The slick comments about us being a couple again were getting on my damn nerves.

****

The next day, the picture people came and so did Kalila and Jamaica. My mom strolled in with my father and brother Kash. Most of the conversations were with me because no one could stand Zahra but my mom and for good reason.

I handed Sasha back to her mother and went to use the bathroom. When I came out Rhythm and Axel were standing at the door. She said he wanted to see his auntie's baby. It's sad that Zahra can't stand his mother because of jealousy and he loved her to death. I pulled her in for a kiss and whispered how much I missed her.

"TiTi Zahra." She looked up and smiled but rolled her eyes when I sat Rhythm on my lap.

"Hey baby. How are you?"

"I'm fine but somebody messed up mommy's room. They cut up everything. Do you know who did it because I saw your car at the house? Did you see the person?" He bombarded her with questions.

"I did it." All of us got quiet. I moved Rhythm off my lap because shit is about to get crazy. Zahra's mom told her to shut the fuck up in a nice way but as usual, her ass didn't listen.

"Why would you do that to mommy?" He was confused as hell.

"Because I hate your mother and if I could kill her, I would."

"OH MY GOD!" My mom shouted. Rhythm tried to jump on the bed but my dad caught her just in time.

"GET MY SON OUTTA HERE!" She screamed and my mother actually took him out. One thing my mom doesn't play is, saying or doing ignorant shit around kids.

"You's a stupid bitch. Why the fuck would you say some dumb shit like that to a kid?"

"Because I do hate her. I hate everything about her." I stared at Rhythm who was tryna calm down.

"Why the fuck did you have to come in our life? Bitch, Kalila is my sister and she's my mother."

"Get off me. I don't care if she just had a baby. I'm about to beat her ass."

"You ain't doing shit." Zahra picked my baby up. She knew like I did, Rhythm wouldn't touch her.

"I'm fine Mr. Garcia. Put me down." He did and she fixed her clothes.

"You acting like you're better than me. Like your pussy good enough for him not to stray. Well guess what?" I knew right then shit was about to be fucked up.

"Last week at the doctors."

"Shut yo ass up Zahra."

"Nah. Fuck you and her."

"Last week we kissed in the doctor's office and I sucked him off." Rhythm looked at me and so did everyone else. I've never been a cheater and they all knew how I felt about Rhythm, well except my mother because she was in denial. I'm sure they're wondering why, the same way I am.

"That's right bitch. Then he took your dumb ass to Mexico to try and cover up his guilt. Bitch, I ain't going nowhere. We got years in." The tears rolling down Rhythm's face fucked me up. I should've never kept this from her knowing the type of person Zahra is. The sad part is she just told me in Mexico how much in love with me, she was.

"Ok then." She walked up on me.

"Here's the keys to your truck, your house in Sayreville and the condo downtown." She dug in her purse to get them.

"Sayreville? Condo?" Zahra questioned and I kept my eyes on Rhythm.

"You should've known about these places since you have time in but let me clear Zahra." She moved closer but I stood in between.

"I'm not gonna cause a scene because it's no need." She said but I wasn't taking a chance. Rhythm was that mad.

"Years in with a nigga don't mean shit as you can tell."

"Whatever."

"Now its whatever because you see I got the keys to his shit but here." She passed them to her and I snatched them

14

right outta Zahra's hand. I wish the fuck I would let her have them.

"You were right about one thing and that's, that you two belong together." She wiped her face, grabbed her purse and walked out with Kalila behind. I tried to go after her but my father told me to give her space. I stared at this bitch and had she not been holding Sasha I probably would've strangled her. My father had to hold me back.

"What's up?" My brother Kommon strolled in smiling.

"What up?" He gave me a hug and something was off. I knew when shit wasn't right with him and he knew too because his smile turned into a slight frown.

"You here to see your niece?"

"My niece?" He questioned.

"Yea. This dumb bitch just had my daughter."

"Your daughter? Nah bro. I'm here to see my daughter."

"Nigga, I ain't no you had a kid. Ma, did you know?" I asked when she stepped in.

"Kommon, you never told me about any kids."
Confusion was written on everyone's face except his and
Zahra's. Then I remembered what Kash said.

"Zahra said she told you it was a chance the baby may
not be yours."

"What the fuck you just say?"

"I told you Kruz but nobody wanted to listen to me."
Kash said sitting in the chair.

"You heard me. Now where's the nurse so we can get a
test done. I'm either the father or the uncle." All I saw was red.

I walked out the room with Kalila holding my hand, hurt, humiliated and embarrassed. I definitely knew about the doctor's appointment but the rest remained a secret until she blasted it. Who knew she hated me so much she'd blurt it out to my child. My poor baby covered his ears and started crying. He was devastated and everyone in the room knew it.

"Come on sweetie." I lifted him up out of Kruz's mom arms. She had the nerve to ask if he's gonna be ok, as if she cares.

"You don't have to worry about this one here."

"Rhythm. I'm..."

"You're what? Sorry." I looked her up and down. This woman was pathetic and I didn't care to hear any fake ass apologies.

"You're not sorry one bit. This is what you wanted right? You did any and everything possible to try and keep them together. Made her weasel back in the house, buy things for the baby and go to doctors' appointments." The insurance

17

guy who left his card at the motel walked past us and went to the bitch's room. How did they know each other?

"Let's go sis." Kalila took my hand in hers.

"I understand why you felt he should go to the doctors but what you should've done is taken the time out to be his mother, and not hers." She sucked her teeth and we walked off. I turned and saw her going in Zahra's room.

"Effff him sis." I laughed at Kalila because I know she wanted to say more and didn't. We really tried our hardest not to curse in front of him.

I placed Axel in the back of the Uber called and put his seatbelt on. Neither of us had a car here and this was our only option unless I got the keys back from Zahra and drove his truck.

I leaned my head on the window and closed my eyes. Why in the hell did I end up falling in love with a man who's clearly not over his ex?

The Uber stopped in front of the house and Kalila helped me pack some things for me and my son. There're a few vacancies at the motel and I asked our boss if I could

18

occupy one. I told him someone broke in my house and I'm scared to stay there. He's cool and pretty much lets me do whatever since I've been working here right outta high school.

I never got the chance to experience college because of my son. I don't regret him one bit, however; I do think about if I'd have a better job had I went to school. Maybe not because Kalila graduated and she still can't get a good paying job no matter how many applications she put out.

"Hey, can I drop Axel off until tomorrow?" I asked his father's mom. She loved my son and hated when I picked him up.

"Yes girl. You don't ever have to ask." I hung up and packed him some games too. The three of us left in my car, I dropped him off at his grandmothers and headed to the motel with my best friend next to me.

I went in the office, spoke to the chick working and grabbed a key to the room next door to the office. The boss stayed here sometimes if he had to work and no one could cover, which is rarely. The room is basically a one-bedroom apartment.

It's actually nice in here, minus the ugly ass picture he has hanging in the living room. It's a big black tiger with blue eyes he said, he had to have. I asked why doesn't he put it in his own house? He said, it was expensive and his wife would kill him if she knew he brought it.

The kitchen is small but big enough for a square table and two chairs. The bathroom is a decent size and the bedroom has a nice set in here, thanks to me. He offered me to stay here a few years ago but I didn't wanna move. I furnished the place and even put an exercise bike in to work out. It's gonna do for now.

I wasn't worried about Ms. Bell losing the house anymore because it's paid off and so is the loan. I'm still waiting to hear back about the person putting all those things in my name. Thankfully, the guy put in for fraud so it's not on my credit report.

I never called the insurance guy and I'm glad I didn't if he's affiliated with Kruz. Not saying he'd do me dirty but I don't need him telling my business.

"You ok Rhythm?" Kalila was sitting on the couch texting when I stepped out the shower.

"Yea. I knew he was too good to be true."

"Rhythm, I'm not taking his side but do you think Zahra did it on purpose?"

"What you mean?" I put lotion in my hands and then my legs.

"She had him going to those appointments probably tryna get them alone. He probably had a moment and didn't mean to mess up."

"Really?"

"I'm just saying. He really does love you and I don't think you should take him back if you don't want too. However; I do believe my sister planned all of this, down to exposing him in front of you."

"Oh. I don't doubt that at all. I just wanna know why did he allow her to even get that far?"

"The only person who can answer that is him." She stood and went to the window.

"Yup and I don't wanna hear the excuses so its best we part ways. Kalila, are you listening?" I asked because she was occupied at the window.

"Bitch, it's those niggas again and they leaving."

"What niggas?" I walked over to where she was and peeked out.

"The ones hiding shit in the room."

"Ok and..." I moved when the van pulled off.

"And they left. Let's go see what they hiding."

"Girl, are you crazy?"

"Yup and so are you? Put your slippers on." I blew my breath, grabbed the key to my room and followed her to the front desk. I told the chick she could take a half hour break because we'll be here. It's the only way we could grab their key and go in the room. It would give us time to go in and come back.

"You ready?" Kalila grabbed my hand and we walked down passed all the doors. We made it to the room, looked around and didn't see any cars coming.

"Hurry up bitch before we get caught." She barked because it was taking time to get in.

"I think they did something to the lock." I kept jiggling the key until the door finally opened. Both of us rushed in and closed the door.

"Shit! Where's the light?" I moved my hands around on the wall and felt a body.

"Really Kalila. Move so I can turn it on."

"Heffa, I'm over here." Her voice came from a different direction and at that very moment, I knew we fucked up coming in here.

"If you're over there, then who is..."

"Didn't we tell you nosy bitches to stay out this room?" His voice sent chills down my spine and not good ones.

CLICK! I felt the cold gun on my temple.

"Rhythm you have to see this shit in the bathroom." Dude turned the lights on and Kalila froze.

"Lord please forgive me for my sins and watch over my son." I said out loud and asked myself, why in the hell did I listen to this crazy ass girl?

K: *Babe, you need to get to the hospital.*

Me: *What's wrong? You ok?*

K: *Yea. Zahra blasted Kruz in front of Rhythm about them sleeping together and it's a mess.*

Me: *A'ight. I'll be there shortly.*

I dropped my girl off earlier to visit her sister and newborn niece. I planned on going in too because it's my boys' baby but other things had to be taken care of. Such as me walking into this restaurant to meet up with Kandy. I'm not going to re kindle no flame or have sex. I'm good with my girl and I'm not tryna lose her again.

"What's the deal? You tryna send yo new nigga after me?" I blurted out the second we made eye contact. She had a seat in the back of the place. It wasn't packed and the few people there seemed to be in their own world.

"Have a seat Jamaica."

"I'm good standing."

"Suit yourself." She picked her fork up and continued eating as if my presence meant nothing. I knocked everything

24

off the table, snatched her up by the shirt and pushed her against the wall.

"You know I'm not into games."

"Jamaica please let me go." She attempted to pry my hands off but it was no use because my grip was tight.

"Tell me what you got planned with him."

"How can I when you have me against the wall?" I released my grip and slammed her hard in the chair.

"Are you ok?" Some woman walked over being nosy.

"Mind your business." She backed away.

"Jamaica, I think you should rethink the divorce. I mean you have much to lose." I gave her a crazy look.

"I ain't got shit to lose. You on the other hand are playing a dangerous game."

"Kalila Bell isn't worth losing?" I put my gun under her chin and my knee in her stomach. I don't give a fuck about her claiming to be being pregnant. It ain't my motherfucking kid.

"What did you do?" She smiled and put her hand on top of mine.

"You think I'm playing?"

25

POW!

"OH MY GOD!" She screamed. I shot her foot and put the gun back under her chin. People were running out the place.

"Let's try this again.

"I didn't do it. He did."

"Speak."

"The guy I'm messing with said I couldn't divorce you because my name attached to yours, held a lot of weight."

"You're not making any sense."

"All I know is he's aware of you putting a gun under my chin."

"Because you told him, not that I care. What does that have to do with anything?"

"He found out about the woman you've been with and at this very moment sent someone to find her." I pushed myself off her and backed away.

"What the fuck you mean?" She tried to nurse her foot that was bleeding profusely but I smacked her hand away.

"One of the guys you have working for you is his cousin and he's looking for her." I smacked the fuck outta her dumb ass.

"This is all your fault."

"Jamaica, I…"

"Bitch don't say a fucking word and you need to pray nothing happens to my girl because if it does, I promise I'll be back for you." I walked out the restaurant and noticed a black truck sitting on the opposite side of the street. Never being the one to show fear, I walked over, tapped on the glass and waited for the window to come down. When it did, I was shocked as hell.

"Tha fuck you doing here? It's a long way from home." I said to my father. He moved back to Jamaica a few years ago because my mom no longer wanted to be here. Unfortunately, she passed away when someone robbed the bank she was in.

"I'm here to kill my ex best friend's daughter."

"What? Why is that?" I was confused as shit, yet; still needed to find my girl. My phone went off and I ignored it for the moment.

"Kandy's mother killed your mom, so it's only right I take someone from them" He blew the smoke out his cigar.

"Pops, you know moms died in a random act of violence." He smirked and handed me an envelope.

"When you live in the world we live in, they're never random acts."

"What's this?"

"Proof that she's involved in your moms killing. Read it over and come see me at the Marriott when you finish doing whatever you're about to do." The window went up and his truck pulled off. I looked down at my phone because it kept going off. There were missed calls from Kruz's father and a text from Kalila. I hauled ass to my car.

"What the fuck is that?" I noticed a van in front of me with a body hanging out. The person pointed something in my direction.

SWISH! I heard and watched as a MANPAD flew in my direction. It's a small anti-aircraft missile used to target helicopters and other small things. Everything happened so fast, I had no other choice but to face the inevitable.

28

BOOM!!!!!

"Come again." I said to my brother Kommon. There's no fucking way he just said, what I think he said.

"Kommon were you sleeping with Zahra too?" My mother asked and I could tell by her facial expression that not only was she disgusted but shocked.

"Yes, but I didn't know."

"Kruz." I heard Zahra and turned to see her gripping Sasha.

"Ms. Bell, please take her out." She stared at me and rushed over to her daughter.

"No mommy. This is my baby." Zahra refused to let Sasha go and she had good reason. The second the baby isn't in her hands, I'm gonna kill her.

"I told you the bitch was nasty."

"Shut up Kash." My mother tried to smack him but my pops blocked her.

All he did is give me space to get over to Kommon. I started beating his ass like a nigga off the street. He tried to fight back but he knew like everyone else, it was no win. Once

30

he hit the ground, my foot connected with his face, back, stomach and anywhere else.

"Kruz, stop it right now." I heard my mother yell. It wasn't until my father used all his strength to lift me up off him.

"Oh my God. Get a doctor in here." My mother dropped to her knees next to Kommon and I turned my attention back to Zahra.

"What's going on in here?" A nurse stepped in, saw my brother on the floor and walked out. I could hear her screaming for a doctor and police.

"We're taking another test."

"Kruz the test proved she's yours." I ran over to Zahra, put my gun on her forehead and cocked it.

"We have the same parents, which means the same blood you dumb bitch. It's no telling if the test is correct."

"Son, put the gun away." Ms. Bell had fear on her face and Zahra had fake ass tears running down hers.

"I wanna kill you so bad right now." I pushed the gun into her forehead and mushed her head into the pillow.

"FREEZE!" I heard and smiled. The cops got here quick.

"Back up slowly sir." I put the gun in my waist, lifted my hands and mouthed the words, *I'm gonna kill you* to her.

"Why you arresting him? Arrest that stupid bitch." Kash walked over to Zahra and hock spit in her face.

"I wish any of you would fucking touch him." It wasn't right for him to do it but I could care less. The cop placed handcuffs on my wrist and escorted me out the room. I saw all the blood on the floor and stepped over.

"Kruz, how could you beat your brother like that." My moms said coming out behind me.

"You don't have shit to say to me." The cop pressed the elevator and told his partner he'd see him at the station. I guess he's taking statements from that dumb bitch.

"Don't speak to me that way." I had to laugh.

"Why not? Huh? Besides finding out my brother fucked my ex, you played a big part in the drama going on. So don't stand there playing victim. Matter of fact, get the fuck out my face."

"Kruz." I heard my pops.

"Nah, because the way I see it is, had she not been so far up Zahra's ass, she would've seen what my ten-year-old brother did. And still, you failed to mention any of it to me." I looked her up and down.

"Remember all that tough shit you were talking at my house? I don't hear it now."

"Son, I didn't know."

"But you knew he came over and took her out. You knew they were supposedly discussing me and what did you do?" She put her head down.

"WHAT THE FUCK DID YOU DO?" I shouted as the elevator binged to let us know it's about to open.

"You ain't do a fucking thing. No phone calls, or even a hint of those two conversing in general."

"Let's go." The cop said and I asked him to give me a minute.

"I'm your son too and regardless of how innocent you claimed it to be, you should've told me." I chuckled a little.

33

"I can't even be that mad at Kommon because he didn't know who she was, but the bitch had to know who he was because we look alike."

"I'm sorry Kruz."

"Save your tired ass fucking apologies and stay the fuck away from me."

"You don't mean that son."

"You know the only reason I didn't come for you is because I could tell you really didn't know but if you did, I promise pops would've had to carry you around the house for the rest of your life."

"THAT'S ENOUGH KRUZ." My mother had tears coming down her face.

"I'm done pops. I think she remembers who the fuck I am now because it's obvious she forgot." The cop and I stepped on and I dared my mother to say another word or try to get on. I was done with her bullshit and everyone else.

"Don't call my phone or attempt to stop by my house or you will regret it." I threw the last threat out before the elevator door closed. I don't care how anyone feels about the way I spoke to my mother. She was dead ass wrong and if no one else would tell her, I did.

"Watch your head." The cop used the palm of his hand and pushed me down a little in the car, closed the door and hopped on the driver's side.

"What the hell is that?" He shouted and I looked out the window to see an explosion. It must've been a few streets over because you could see debris flying.

"All available units report to the south side. All available units please report to the south side." You heard different cops responding to the call as he drove me down to the station. I wonder what the fuck happened over there.

****

"You got bailed out." I stared at the cop, rose to my feet and walked out behind him.

"Who paid it?" He didn't get a chance to answer because Drew turned around.

"What up boss?" The lady at the desk handed me my belongings. I emptied the bag and noticed the baby bracelet. It

35

made me wanna go to the hospital and kill Zahra. I should've done it before the cops got there

"Shit. How you know I was here?" He glanced over at the captain's door. He didn't have to say a word.

"You need anything?"

"Nah. Just give me a ride to my house."

"Before we go, I think we need to stop by the motel." I sat in his car and put my seatbelt on. This nigga drives like a maniac.

"For?" I pulled my phone out to call and check on Rhythm. I felt like shit for falling victim to Zahra that day in the hospital and planned on doing whatever possible to make her forgive me.

"Some shit went down." I scrolled down my phone and noticed a text message from Kalila. It came at the same time shit went down with my brother. I opened it up.

Kalila: *Kruz, I can't reach Jamaica. Please get to the motel. Someone's tryna kill me and Rhythm.* My heart dropped because if Drew's telling me something went down there and she's saying someone is tryna kill them, it has to go together.

When we pulled up, the place appeared to be quiet. No cops or anyone running around. I hopped out the car, banged on the door and noticed the dead body right away. His body was full of bullets. The guys in charge of this spot, stood there looking stupid.

"Tha fuck happened?" I barked and walked in the bathroom to see if the girls were here. I instantly got pissed seeing the different weapons spread out.

"We found him this way." I stepped over the guy and went to the bed where I saw something shiny. I lifted the bracelet I purchased Rhythm at Tiffany's.

"Where's the chicks at?"

"Boss, there wasn't anyone here when we showed up."

"Fuck!" I ran out and down to the office. I rung the bell and when no one came out, I kicked the door down.

"Who are you?" Some chick jumped off the loveseat.

"Where's Rhythm and Kalila?"

"I'm not telling you shit." I ran up on her.

"I think you are." I slammed her face in the wall.

"She's at the hospital."

"What happened to her?" I threw her on the ground. Fear was all over her face and I didn't give a fuck. Who told her stupid ass to get smart?

"I don't know."

"Don't play with me." I kicked her in the side.

"Please stop." Drew pulled me back and helped her up.

"I apologize for my boss. He's just tryna find out what happened to his girl."

"I went to lunch for a half hour. I came back and next thing I know, an ambulance pulls up. I'm sorry. I really don't know what happened."

"If I find out you're lying Sarah, I'ma come back and murk you."

"Here." I saw Drew pass her money. I wasn't giving her shit.

"Boss, you gotta relax. You can't go around fucking people up."

"Rhythm was in the room." He met her a few times and like everyone else, he knew how strong my feelings were.

"You sure? I don't see the guys allowing her inside." I lifted the bracelet.

"I brought this for her and even if she was mad at me, she's not gonna drop it there." He nodded and sped to the hospital. I had no business returning here.

We walked in and asked the receptionist where her room was. It felt like my heart was racing with each step I took. The second I opened the door, Kalila ran over and hugged me. I couldn't help but notice blood on her clothes. I glanced over at Drew and he took her out the room. Anything linking her to the room needed to be destroyed.

"Is she ok?" I asked some woman who favored her.

"Who are you?"

"Her man. Who are you?"

"Her mother and you don't look like Axel."

"Axel?"

"Yea. Her fiancé."

"Say what?"

"They're getting married next year, which is how I know you can't be her man." I nodded and backed out the room.

"Hey. Is she ok?" Zahra's mom asked. I knew she'd be down here once she heard.

"I don't know. You have to ask her fiancé."

"Fiancé?" She was as confused as I.

"Do me a favor?"

"Kruz..." She tried to speak but I stopped her.

"Let her know I came to apologize and beg her to take me back but I'm good now. She can live happily ever after with the nigga for all I care."

I stormed out, saw a cab dropping someone off and hopped in it. Today is not my fucking day.

I walked in the bathroom and my mouth hit the floor. There were chainsaws, a machete and long knives in the tub. The sink held a few guns and zip ties on the counter. I almost threw up staring at the two fingers. I knew they were from a female because of the polish on them.

I ran out to tell Rhythm and some nigga had his gun on her temple. She recited a prayer and asked for God to watch over her son just as he bust her in the head with it. Instead of running towards them unarmed, I backed away in the bathroom and closed the door. I paced it for a few seconds, that felt like hours and remembered my phone. I sent a message to Jamaica and Kruz in case they weren't together, begging them to get here fast.

BOOM! BOOM! I heard him kicking the door and panic took over again. I had to calm myself down before I ended up dead like the people in scary movies.

BOOM! BOOM! He kicked it again and the door flew open. I reached in the sink where those guns were and shot.

41

POW! POW! POW! POW! His body dropped in front of me and fell forward.

SHIT! I hopped over him and ran to check on Rhythm. Her head was bleeding and her shirt had been ripped. I know this pink wasn't about to rape her.

"Rhythm, wake up." I patted her face over and over.

"Wake up sis." I put my hands on her shoulders and damn near shook her to death. Why isn't she waking up? Panic set in even more. How would I be able to tell her son, his mm died following me we had no business being?

"RHYTHMMMMM!" I started crying harder.

"What happened?" Her eyes were barely open but a bitch was happy she wasn't dead.

"I'll tell you in the room. We have to get out of here." She looked down at her clothes and then at me.

"Again, I'll tell you in the room." She nodded and slid off the bed. You could tell how dizzy she was. I placed her arm around my neck and I had her waist.

"You didn't leave anything behind, did you?" I felt for my phone and made sure I had the key to put back.

"No. I don't think so."

I opened the room door and sat her in the kitchen at the table. I left and went to return the key and smiled as the worker walked in. I told her no one checked in and if she needed us we were in the room.

"You ok?" I closed the door, ran to the bathroom to grab a wash rag, wet it and wiped down her face.

"Sis, the gash is deep. You're gonna have to..." I never finished because she passed the hell out. I stared down at my phone and realized Jamaica or Kruz never responded to the text. With no one to call, I did the only thing necessary, and that's call an ambulance.

****

"Is she ok?" Her mom rushed in and rubbed her hair. They may not get along but she's still her mom and its only right I called.

"I don't know yet." My knees were to my chest and as I sat in the chair waiting on the results to come in. I know Rhythm is going to kill me for contacting her but I had no choice. My mother was upstairs with my dumb ass sister and the doctor wouldn't release any information unless I could prove we were related.

"What happened?"

"We were walking outside the motel and someone attacked her."

"Attacked her? I told Rhythm a long time ago to leave the motel and get a real job." I sucked my teeth because she really be tryna act bougie. She may have moved out the projects years ago but she still from the hood

"She can do so much better with her life." I totally understood her prospective on what she thinks is good for her child, however; had it not been for her rich husband, she'd be doing some crazy job too. I couldn't stand people who looked down on others. It's one of the reasons Rhythm didn't fuck with her now.

"Are you mom?" The doctor walked in with a nurse.

"Yes. She's her sister so I'm not understanding why you couldn't release any information to her." The one thing I can say about her mom is, she respected our bond no matter what.

"She didn't have any ID."

"Since when do hospitals or better yet doctors start asking for someone's ID?"

"I'm sorry ma'am. We have to be careful and..."

"Whatever. What's going on with my child?" He proceeded to tell her and she let him have it.

"It's funny how you're about to release her information to me and haven't asked for ID?"

"You said, you were her mom."

"And she told you, she was her sister." His face turned red because he knew his ass was dead wrong.

"I'm sorry ladies. It won't happen again."

"It better not or I will sue the hell out of this hospital. And don't ask me for what, I'm sure my lawyer can draft up a few things." He nodded and she gave him a fake smile. I put my head down laughing.

"Ms. Mitchell suffered a concussion, and the laceration required six stitches. The bump on her head will go down eventually, as well as the black eye. Also, I'm not sure if anyone knows but there was skin under her nails. Was she in a fight?" Her mom and the doctor stared at me. The nigga must've really tried to rape her. I figured if skin was under her nails, she came to and tried to fight him and he knocked her back out. What a fucking bitch ass nigga. It's exactly why he dead now.

"Sort of." Neither of them asked me to speculate and I'm glad.

"Last but not least, she's pregnant."

"Oh my God. I'm going to be a grandmother again." I rolled my eyes at her dramatic ass. Axel barely knows her and she pretending to be excited.

"The reason she's still asleep is because the hit must've been pretty hard. We gave her a low dose of Demerol and Tylenol to try and alleviate pain.

"It's not gonna hurt the baby, right?" He told us no, shook our hands and stepped out.

"Hey." I stood when Kruz and some other guy stepped in. One look at me and he had the guy take me out. I didn't know why until we got to his car and he threw a t-shirt in over mine.

"Jamaica will handle the rest." I snapped my neck. How the hell did he know about my man?

"The whole crew know who you two are so don't be surprised."

"Ummm ok." I noticed Kruz storming out the hospital.

"Is everything ok?" I asked and he told me to tell Rhythm to lose his number. I had no idea what her mom said but it must be bad if he's upset.

I stepped back in the room and saw Rhythm's stepdad standing there. Anger filled my face and her mom saw me. She knew how reckless my mouth is and hurried him out. He's the reason they don't speak now and she had the nerve to invite him up. *The fucking nerve.* I closed the door, turned the light off and made myself comfortable in that tight ass chair.

When that shit came in my direction, I swore my life was over. It flew past me and before I could turn around, the explosion rocked my car, the ground and most likely the buildings. I turned to see if it hit my pops truck and couldn't tell because shit was everywhere. There are a lotta things you can get away from, but a small missile ain't one of them.

I hopped out my ride and ran over to the restaurant hoping Kandy died in it. Unfortunately, she was running or should I say limping to her car. I thought about finishing what I started and stopped myself because the person who shot the missile hadn't pulled off yet which is weird.

People were running outta places screaming, some crying and others bleeding. Buildings were in shambles and the motherfucker who did it stuck around. Where the hell they do that at? My mind was in overdrive and all I could think of is who the person is and if he came to take me out.

"Yo!" I answered my phone without looking.

"Get back in your car." I turned around after hearing my father's voice. How the hell did he know where I'm at.

"I mean it Jamaica. He's not done and I need you outta there."

"What you mean he's not done?"

"Just go and check on your girl. She's at the hospital." I stopped short, ran back to my car and sped off. I totally forgot Kalila text me about her and Rhythm. What does he mean she's at the hospital? I pressed Kruz number on the way to see if he were ok as well.

"What up?" He didn't sound upset.

"You good?"

"Yea. Why you ask that?"

"I got a text from Kalila saying Zahra told Rhythm about the doctor's appointment." Of course, I knew what happened. He had a weak moment for his ex but I did tell him he should've told Rhythm when we were in Mexico. At least she wouldn't have been able to leave.

"Zahra couldn't wait to mention it but get this." I pulled in at the hospital and found a parking spot.

"Kommon comes in asking if he's a father or niece."

"Huh? I ain't know he had kids on the way." I hit the alarm and stepped in the revolving doors.

"That's what I said until Kash's comment at the house popped in my head. Evidently, the bitch was fucking him too." I stopped and asked him to repeat himself. When he did, I couldn't believe it. Him and Kommon may not be close but they knew to stay away from one another's chicks.

"Evidently, he didn't know and told her she needed to let me know."

"Damn bro. You ok?"

"It's fucking me up because not only is she my ex and he's my brother, but would I really be bothered if the baby ends up being my niece?"

"I don't even know what to say." I asked the nurse for Kalila room when she said no one is there by that name, I asked for Rhythm. I had no idea what her last name is but the chick still gave me the info.

"Let me see what's up with Kalila and I'll hit you back."

"A'ight and do me a favor."

"What's that?" I stepped in and smiled at my girl knocked out on the side of her best friends bed.

"Tell Rhythm to lose my number."

"What did I miss?"

"Man, the bitch is engaged and before you ask, her mother had no problem giving out the information."

"I'll be there soon." I hung up and put the phone in the clip. I can tell in my boy voice he's fucked up over the shit with Zahra but now Rhythm too. Yea, we need some drinks.

"Hey ma." I tapped Kalila on her leg. She opened her eyes, stood and hugged me tight.

"You good?" She nodded yes.

"Why are y'all here?" I could tell by her expression she didn't wanna say.

"Outside." I grabbed her hand and walked out.

"Speak." She started telling me the story and mad isn't the word for how I felt. Why in the hell would she do something stupid?

"Let me get this right." I paced back and forth.

"You persuaded your best friend to go in a room that you knew was probably dangerous, saw weapons in the bathroom, the guy pulled a gun on her, you think he tried to rape her, locked yourself in the bathroom and came out shooting."

"Jamaica, I'm sorry. I just wanted to see what they were hiding."

"WHY? IT WASN'T YOUR FUCKING BUSINESS." Her eyes got big. In the two years we've been together I've never yelled at her. I gripped her arms and moved away from the benches she was sitting on.

"Do you have any fucking idea the type of danger you were in? What if they killed your friend or both of you? What if the cops showed up and took your ass to jail?" I was so mad, I had to catch myself from punching the window. I sent a text to Drew asking if everything were ok.

"Jamaica, I didn't know..."

"Who the fuck cares Kalila? That was someone else's room you went into. Regardless if it were bad shit going down in there or not, you had no business going in." She started crying and I wanted to feel bad and couldn't.

"Do I bring you around my street life?"

"No."

"Do I put you in danger?"

"No."

"Then why in the fuck would you put yourself and best friend in danger? What if she died? How would her son feel?" She cried harder.

"Yo, I'm out."

"Don't leave baby. I'm sorry."

"The shit you did was reckless and now I have to clean it up."

"Wait! You know those people?"

"Questions like that don't need to be answered." I headed towards my car.

"Why not Jamaica?"

"Because it's none of your business. The less you know, the better. Go inside and be with your friend."

"Jamaica don't you.-" I ran up on her.

"Don't even think about causing a scene or tryna get mad at me to cover up, your fuck up."

"I wasn't..."

"Go check on your friend Kalila and I'll see you when I see you."

"You're breaking up with me?"

"Go inside Kalila, DAMN. WHY CAN'T YOU LISTEN?" I barked.

"Well I guess it's time for me to go."

"It is." I gestured with my head for her to go in.

I hated to yell but she wasn't getting it. I told her in so many words the people are mine and she continued going on and on.

After she went in and was outta sight, I met up with Drew at the motel, made sure everything was handled and told Kruz to meet us at the bar. It didn't take long for him to come and when he did, all of us got fucked up. We ended up closing the bar and took an Uber home.

****

"Tha fuck you doing Kalila. Got damn." I gripped the sheets tight as fuck while she deep throated me. I came home from the bar and went straight to sleep but it didn't last long because she woke me up. It didn't help being horny too.

Her hands slid up and down my dick as her tongue went in circles over the tip. My nut was coming up fast and it's probably because the liquor is still in my system. Her other hand juggled my balls and the pressure to cum kept building. She spit and my ass lost all fucking control.

"FUCK, K!" I let her suck everything I had out and laid there breathing hard as hell.

"Fuck me hard daddy." She whispered in my ear and grinded her soaking wet pussy on top of me. My dick grew in no time.

"I don't feel you inside yet. Mmmm daddy fuck me." I squeezed her ass, flipped her over, lifted her legs back to her ears and pushed myself in.

"AHHHHHHH!" Her nails dug in my arms as she tried fucking me from the bottom.

"Damn she gushy ma." The sounds from her cumming was loud and the amount seeping out covered my entire dick.

"They say pregnant pussy will do it." I stopped and turned the light on. She already had tears sliding down her face.

"How far?"

"Three months." I smiled, kissed her lips and got on my knees to please her.

"Jamaica, I can't take anymore." After she came for the third time, I reentered and went slow.

"That's why you calling me daddy?" She wrapped her arms around my neck.

"You know I never call you that."

"You're about to be my baby mom. Fuck, this pussy so damn good." I turned her over to keep from cumming fast.

"Throw it back." Once she did, the two of us fucked like rabbits throughout the night. It was nonstop and when we did finish, she complained about being sore and holding out for a few days. *Yea right.*

"I'm sorry Jamaica." She was laying on my chest.

"How's Rhythm?"

"She woke up after you left expecting to see Kruz."

"Why is that when she left the hospital mad about the shit with your sister?" Kruz told me she texted him while we were out and how he blocked her. I would've too if someone I loved was engaged.

"She still loves him and after I mentioned the stuff with Zahra, all she wanted to do is be there for him."

"Well it's a wrap for him. He don't wanna be bothered."

"But why?" My phone went off as I was about to tell her. It was a message from my dad asking to meet up in a few days. I responded, put the phone down and pulled her closer. I'll discuss the shit with her later.

"This is what you're doing?" I stood in front of Kruz at the club. He had some chick on his arm. I haven't seen him in two weeks and when I do he has a woman in his face.

"What you want Rhythm?" How he gonna have an attitude when I'm the one he's ignoring?

The day I left the hospital, I went to his place and shockingly the code to the gate was changed, which meant all the locks were too. But why? I'm the one who got embarrassed and humiliated in front of everyone, not him. Well, I guess he did eventually but it wasn't because of me.

Anyway, I called him over and over because not only did I wanna speak to him, so did my son. He called himself blocking me and the only reason I didn't completely black out is because Kalila did take Axel to see him whenever he asked.

I give him credit for not walking out on my son. It doesn't mean he won't but for now, he's not. Shit, a few times Kash stopped by with Kalila at the motel to grab clothes for Axel to stay the night. He didn't understand why Kruz wasn't speaking to me either.

I asked Kalila if she knew and Jamaica won't tell. Any time she tried to ask, something would come up. Whatever it is, can't be that bad because I haven't slept with anyone else. And I know for a fact this child I'm carrying is his.

It's fucked up what Zahra did and I truly believe if the cops hadn't shown up, Kruz would've killed her. It's one thing to cheat but another to do it with his brother. After being with Kruz, I can't even explain why she'd cheat. He's definitely a good man and the sex is amazing.

"Rhythm? That's a weird name."

"It is right?" He had the nerve to entertain her comment.

"Bitch, you don't know me. Keep talking and I'ma beat your ass." The girl looked scared as hell and he laughed with his ignorant ass. Here he is with a chick who's scary and letting me say whatever.

"Kruz, you have thirty seconds to meet me outside or I promise I'm gonna be the ratchet bitch you hate."

"You're not my woman so I don't give a fuck what you do." He sipped the beer in his hand.

"Ok, so I can go fuck any of these niggas here?" I waved my hand around the club. His face became tight. I smiled on the inside because it meant he still had some sort of feelings for me.

"Look Rhythm." The bitch gave me a fake smile and continued talking.

"We are tryna have a good time and you're bothering us. Ain't that right baby?" She placed her hand on his cheek and stood on her tippy toes to kiss him.

WHAP! I punched her in the face and threw her on the ground. She tried to get up and I continued hitting her until he lifted me off.

"Look what you have me doing Kruz." He carried me out the front door and placed me on my feet.

"I don't have you doing a damn thing and you know I don't play that ghetto shit."

"Why have you been avoiding me?"

"Does it matter?"

"Yes, it matters. I wanted to make sure you were ok." I moved in close and wrapped my hands around his waist.

"Why? Don't you have another nigga to sit up under?" I backed away and looked at him.

"I know you didn't just call me a ho."

"If the shoe fits."

"Who are you?"

"What?" He folded his arms across his chest.

"Where is the Kruz I fell in love with? The one who promised to never hurt me? The one who swore he'd never touch his ex again and did it anyway? The one I woke up looking for and was nowhere to be found? What happened to him? This arrogant asshole in front of me is the man, I originally met. The one I couldn't stand."

"I've always been here Rhythm, you were just too caught up to see it."

"Caught up?" I scoffed up a laugh.

"I was caught up alright. Caught up with a lying, piece of shit who cheated on me with a bitch who fucked his brother." His entire demeanor changed.

"Oh, you mad now? Huh? You knew the bitch cheated, couldn't stand her, wanted to kill her and still let her suck you

61

off and kiss you. What, you missed her? I wasn't fucking you right? I mean what was it?" He didn't say shit. I saw his fist balling up.

"I stuck around when your mother tried to run me off. I planned on sticking around even after she destroyed my room over you. I decided to forgive you for slipping up this one time and for what? You to say fuck me and call me a ho."

"Go the fuck home Rhythm."

"I'll go home when the fuck I feel like it." He reached out fast as hell and grabbed my hair. The grip was serious.

"Don't bring your ass around me again." He forced me to my car. I opened the door, sat, locked it and backed up. He started walking across the street.

"Don't you worry about it nigga. I'm gonna make sure another man feels this good ass pussy."

"Tha fuck you say?"

"Doesn't matter now does it? Go be with your new bitch because I'm gonna be with my new nigga. I'm gonna suck his dick so good, he'll be asking for my hand in marriage." I didn't realize I was pushing my luck until he was on the passenger side with a gun under my chin. *I swore, I locked the doors.*

"Talk that shit now Rhythm."

"This don't scare me." I pointed to the gun. He cocked it back and smiled.

"That might." I chuckled, pressed down on the gas and sped down the street.

"Go faster." I thought he would tell me to slow down but nope. He removed the gun and stared at the road.

"If we die at least neither of us will feel it." I started slowing down and looked over at him. When we got to a corner, I pressed on the brakes real hard and both of us went forward. My chest banged into the steering wheel and my head hit the window. He looked over at me.

"You should've put your seatbelt on." He lifted his with his thumb to show he had it on. I could've smacked him.

"GET OUT!" I lifted my feet up and turned. I started kicking him hard as I could.

WHOOP! WHOOP! I snapped my head to the back and three cop cars were behind me.

"GET OUT THE CAR NOW!" I looked at him.

"Don't look at me. I'm an innocent person in all this."

"Kruz, are you serious?"

"Ma'am get outta the car now before I tase you." The car door swung open and my body almost hit the ground.

"Officer, why am I being pulled over?" I asked finally getting on my feet.

"Did you really just ask me that?"

"Ugh Yea." I crossed my arms.

"You were doing ninety-seven miles an hour in a twenty-five."

"That's pretty fast Rhythm." Kruz was getting a kick outta this shit.

"He made me."

"Yea right." The cop placed handcuffs on me and put me in the back of his car.

"Are you ok sir? Do you need the hospital?"

"Why the fuck are you asking him? I'm the one with a knot on my head and probably a chest contusion."

"We'll get to you later miss. Right now, this innocent man needs to be tended to." Kruz looked in the back seat and had a big grin on his face. He stood next to the car and spoke through the barely cracked window.

"I bet yo ass don't do that dumb shit again."

"Fuck you."

"You did and it's the exact reason you're mad. Tryna kill me because another bitch about to ride this ride." He grabbed his dick. I made sure the door was locked this time.

"And another nigga about to eat this juicy pussy. I'ma ride the hell outta his face too." He got pissed all over again.

"Officer can you take me away now? This innocent man is harassing me. I'd like to file a restraining order on him." The cop pulled off before he could respond and thank goodness he did. I saw the other officers tryna hold him back. He got the nerve to be mad after talking all that shit.

****

"Do you need a ride to the hospital?" The cop asked after I got bailed out on my own R&R. I've never been arrested or sent to jail in my life. Kruz had me all the way fucked up.

65

"No thanks." I stepped out the police station looking around for him just in case he waited for me with his petty ass.

"Bitch, who you looking for?" I jumped hearing Kalila.

"Nobody. Take me to the hospital please."

"Oh hell no. Why the fuck didn't they take you? You're pregnant and..." I just broke down in tears.

"You didn't tell him, did you?"

"No."

"Rhythm."

"No sis. I went there to see if we could talk, things went left and he taunted me about sleeping with someone else. I swear, I planned on telling him but it wasn't necessary."

"What you mean it's not necessary? It's his baby. Wait! It is his right?" I rolled my eyes at her.

"I'm just saying. He calling you a ho and shit. I thought maybe he knew something I didn't." I gave her the finger and wiped my eyes when we pulled up at the ER.

"Oh shit." Kalila stopped and grabbed my hand.

"Let's go to a different hospital."

"Why?" I followed her gaze and sucked my teeth. This nigga was inside with the bitch I beat up in the club.

"Fuck them. Watch this." I signed in with the receptionist and found a seat on the other side.

"Girl, look at what he text me. Damn, I can't wait to see him." Kalila and I were cracking up until we felt a presence in front of us.

"Ummm, you're not supposed to be within fifty feet of me." I handed him a piece of paper out my purse. I don't have a restraining order on him and I can't even tell you what's on the one I gave him. I just snatched it out my purse to make it seem real.

"I don't give a fuck about a piece of paper."

"Oh you're above the law huh? One of the guys who kill and harass women even after they tell you to stay away." He laughed and bit down on his lip.

"Bye Kruz. Your bitch is waiting over there for you." He kneeled down in front of me.

"I don't even know why I'm playing this game with you but I will. Just know, you won't win." I rolled my eyes.

67

"Three things and I'm out." He forced me to look at him.

"One... I brought her here because she started to press charges on you and I refuse to let Axel be without his mother."

"Thank you. I guess." Sarcasm dripped from my mouth.

"Two... I literally just met the bitch an hour before you got there. I had no plans on fucking her, but now I have to because you were being ratchet and it's the only way I can keep her quiet."

"I bet."

"I offered money but it's dick she wants so it's your fuck up." He stood and towered over me.

"And three... Let another nigga tell me he smelled the soap you wash in, and I'm gonna snap your fucking neck in front of your mother." He shrugged his shoulders and walked away. I stormed over and pushed him in the back.

"Let's Go Rhythm." Kalila shouted on my way over. The chick jumped up and stood by security. I noticed the black eye and scared look on her face.

68

"Don't you dare threaten me over the same shit you're about to do."

"You heard what the fuck I said." He sat down.

"Fuck you and stay away from me." He smirked and that only pissed me of more.

"I hate you. I hate I ever met you." I punched him in the chest and caught him a few times in the face. He grabbed my wrist and pushed me against the wall.

"Calm the fuck down." He waited a few seconds, let my arms go and wiped my eyes.

"Rhythm Mitchell?" The triage nurse called. I walked up to the chick.

"I'm sorry for what happened. If you become his main chick, please keep him away from me." I can be a grown woman about my shit and admit I was wrong. I didn't have to apologize but she did nothing for me to attack her.

"Rhythm." He called out and I gave him the finger.

"You ok?" Kalila asked shaking her head.

"Perfect." I sat with the triage nurse and tried my hardest to hold the tears in.

69

"When we leave, I'm going to stay in one of my mom's apartments." My stepfather owned so much re estate it's ridiculous.

I could've stayed in one of them years ago but him and I couldn't stand one another. He didn't want kids and basically forced my mother to put me out, which is why Axel got us a place right outta high school.

My mother was so money hungry she did whatever he said. Axel barely knows her because she was too scared to bring him over, let alone spend time with her. Now all of a sudden, she's excited to be a grandmother. *Like bitch, you been one.*

"Ok." I followed the nurse upstairs to the labor and delivery floor and stayed for a few hours. Once they gave me the ok to leave, we got in the car, went to the motel, packed all my things and I had her drop my off to my car.

"You gotta be fucking kidding me." This guy Teddy was standing there with a few other guys. He was very aggressive and persistent one night at the hotel. You would think the nigga was a rapist by the way he acted. If I didn't promise to contact he cops, he probably would've tried something.

"Get in your car and pull off." Kalila said and watched as I did it. Something about the way Teddy stared at me felt off. I wonder if Kruz mentioned him approaching me. Oh well, I'm over everyone.

Zahra

"How dare you show your face on my doorstep?" Mrs. Garcia had an evil look on her face.

WHAP! She smacked the fuck outta me and I stumbled back with Sasha in my hand. She reached, took the car seat and sat her down on the porch.

I hadn't seen her or anyone else in the family since the fiasco at the hospital. I thought shouting out the shit with Kruz and I, would be the only surprise but when Kommon stepped in the room, all hell broke loose.

I sent him a text to take a test but I damn sure didn't expect him to come right away. Granted, he wanted to know but he could've waited. I saw the hurt and anger on Kruz's face. It wasn't my intention for him to ever find out and if the baby came back as Kommon's, I would've fled for sure.

That same day, Kruz parents cursed me out so bad, my mother had to step in and ask them to leave. They had no problem doing so but not before calling the doctor in and requesting a DNA test for Sasha. They were able to get Kommon's straight from the ER Kruz sent him to. And Kruz

72

came up the next day to take his. One of the nurses I know said, he waited all day for the test results. He didn't want anyone altering them.

Luckily, my daughter Sasha did belong to him. I thought it would've made Kruz visit but he refused. I called and sent photos and got no response. It didn't dawn on me that I'm most likely blocked. He can be pissed all he wants, however; our daughter has nothing to do with it.

He's always been stubborn but this is ridiculous. He hasn't even checked on her through my sister that I know of. She didn't tell me if he did, but then again, she's still team Rhythm who I still hate. If I could kill her, I really would. I messed up by saying it in front of Axel, who by the way won't come over or even speak to me anymore.

Unfortunately, I had to move back home with my mother for the moment until the condo I purchased went through at closing. Sadly, it's not for another two weeks and it can't come fast enough. Between my mother and sister, I can't get a break. Yes, they help with my daughter but the sarcasm and smart remarks I can do without.

"I don't know if Kruz told you but Sasha is his. None of you have seen her since the hospital and I think it's wrong." She stepped in my face.

"What's wrong is you making me do any and everything possible to try and make my son be with you, knowing the whole time you've been with my other son." I put my head down in shame.

"What's even crazier, is Kommon never met you and when he did, you failed to mention the relationship between you and his brother." I couldn't respond to anything she said because it was all true.

"Do you know my own son refuses to speak to me over this shit you started? My other son is laid up at home because his brother almost killed him. Yet; you bring your whorish ass to my house questioning why no one has called to see this child. A child made in deceit and betrayal."

"She is Kruz's." She laughed.

"That may be true but her father's paternity should've never been in question. Neither should you have slept with her

74

uncle." She opened the screen door, snatched the baby bag off my shoulder and slammed the door in my face.

"Open this damn door and give me my baby." I started banging on it and stepped back when his father opened it.

"Get yo trifling ass from in front of my house."

"I'm not leaving my baby." He walked on the porch.

"You don't really have a choice, now do you?" He towered over me and I almost shit myself. This man had hate all over his face.

"Call me when I can return." He didn't say anything as I hopped in my car. I bet she won't come over here anymore.

****

"How's my baby?" My mom took her out my arms when she walked in from work. It's been two weeks since Sasha visited her other grandparents and I meant what I said about her not visiting. I have not taken her back there and don't plan on it. If Kruz decides he wants to see Sasha, he can come get her.

"Ok that's it. We are outta here for good."

I closed on my condo yesterday and hired movers the next day. I didn't have furniture here but my clothes and all the stuff Sasha has, was in the basement. I had them follow me to the storage unit where all my old furniture was. I may have given up the place but I kept everything. I could start over but with no Kruz in my life and only one job, I had to start budgeting.

"Did you pay the babysitter?" She asked about her friend Stacey who kept Sasha when I had things to do. She's gonna watch her next week when I go back to work.

I'm no longer a traveling nurse and found an opening at the local hospital. I couldn't leave my child for days at a time.

"Yea, I paid her."

"Good because it's not my job to do it." This is the shit I'm talking about.

"Don't roll your eyes at me. You have money so there's no need for me to be helping you."

"Why not? Your other daughter's boyfriend paid all your loans off, right? You no longer have debt in your name."

"That's my business and don't you dare think I'm supposed to mess up my credit and pay your bills because of it. What the hell is wrong with you?"

"I'm just saying. You have it now."

"And I've taken care of you and her since you been staying here. Buying food, letting you use my electric, water, heat and I even brought your ungrateful ass takeout when I wanted it. Let's not forget you haven't spent a got damn dime on Sasha since she's been born."

"Yes, I have."

"No you haven't. Your sister had to get Sasha a car seat because you didn't have one and couldn't leave the hospital without it. Diapers, bottles, blankets and anything else she needed, one of us got. So don't sit your fake bougie ass over there pretending you've done a damn thing for her. This outfit she has on now was brought by the woman you hate the most."

I stared down at the pink Jordan dress with sneakers to match.

"Excuse me."

"*Excuse me.*" She mocked me.

"After all the stupid shit you did and said to Rhythm's son, she still went out and brought things for Sasha and you know why?" I started taking the outfit off.

"Because she considers Sasha as her niece."

"I don't know why. We're not related and even if she is with my child's father, she'll never be the stepmother. I won't have it." My mother shook her head in disgust.

"One... They aren't even speaking to each other. And two... whoever the woman is that he does decide to be with ain't about to let you rain on her parade so get ready for it."

"What you mean they're not speaking?"

"Is that all you heard?" I grabbed the pink pajama set I know my sister brought out the bag and put it on her.

"They're going through some things right now but I have faith in their love."

"You can't be ok with those two being a couple."

"She has never been your friend Zahra so stop pretending that's what happened. You're mad he fell in love with another woman and it happens to be your sisters' best friend."

"I wouldn't call what they're doing love." She smirked and stood.

"You have no idea how deep the love runs between them."

"Four years is a long time to get over someone."

"And Rhythm told you, time in means nothing."

"Maybe not to her."

"To you too. He gave her the key to places you didn't even know about. He took her on shopping sprees and vacations. Neither of them are going anywhere, trust me." She opened the front door and told me to go.

"I'll see you later baby." She kissed Sasha on the cheek.

"Are you coming to see our new place?"

"For what? You to show off the things you can afford and I can't."

"Ma."

"Bye Zahra. I'll see you later." She closed the door and I placed Sasha in her car seat.

"Wait!" I heard and looked to see Kalila running up.

"Hey aunties baby." I walked around to the driver's

side not paying attention and I should have.

"Let me grab Sasha first." Kalila said when we pulled in front of her mom's house. Zahra was about to get in her car.

"You better hurry up." I snatched the hair scrunchy out the cup holder and put my hair up.

"Lord forgive me. This is my last fight while I'm carrying." I opened the car door, ran up on Zahra, tapped her on the shoulder and beat the breaks off that bitch.

"Don't... you... ever in your fucking life... tell my son... you hate and wanna kill me." I shouted as I banged her head into the side of her door.

"Beat her ass Rhythm." I heard a few people behind me shouting. No one and I mean no one liked Zahra.

"You want Kruz so bad."

BAM! I kicked her in the face.

"You can have him."

BAM! I kicked her in the stomach and slammed her head against the car one last time before backing up.

"DAMNNNNNNNN!" Kids were recording and yelling she got her ass whooped.

81

"Stay the fuck away from my son." I was about to hit her one more time just because, but someone grabbed my arm.

"That's enough Rhythm."

"Oh shit. It's Jamaica and Kruz." I turned and sure enough it was.

"Kalila you let this go on?"

"Jamaica, don't start no shit with me." She handed Sasha to Kruz and for a moment, I enjoyed watching him hold her. You could tell he loved her even though Zahra did dumb shit.

"I'm just saying the baby here and..."

"And she deserved it after saying that shit to my nephew." He put his hands up as Kruz continued staring.

"I'll see you later Kalila." I walked over to my car.

"Make that the last time you attack her when my daughter is here."

"Fuck you nigga."

"You heard what the fuck I said."

"And you heard me but in case you didn't." I stepped to him.

"Fuck you." He mushed me in the forehead.

"If you weren't holding her, I'd kick you in the dick because it's probably the only place I know my hit would hurt."

"How's daddy's girl?" He ignored me and kissed Sasha.

"Move nigga." He had the nerve to sit his big ass on my car. I saw Jamaica and Kalila shaking their head.

"What is wrong with you?"

"Nothing. I'm having a moment with my daughter and you're disrupting us."

"Why can't you do it on her car?"

"This one is better."

"Jamaica can you please get your petty friend away from my car?"

"Y'all two need to make up and cut all this bullshit out." I sucked my teeth and folded my arms.

"He has a new bitch and I got a new man. Therefore; we won't be rekindling a damn thing." He stood and walked Sasha over to Kalila. This was my chance to leave.

I hopped in the car, started it and put it in drive. This nigga stood right in front of me. I looked on the side of me and around to make sure no kids were outside, stepped on the gas and sped around his body. I could've hit him but he may actually kill me.

CRASH! I turned to see my back windshield busted out and then my tires blew. This nigga stood in the middle of the street aiming to shoot again. I stopped and backed up even with the blown-out tires.

"YOU FUCKING HAPPY NOW? DOES THIS MAKE YOU FEEL BETTER KRUZ?" I left the car running and ran in the house crying like a baby. I hauled ass upstairs in my old room and fell on the bed.

"You do know when y'all make up, he's gonna make it hurt when you walk."

"He left me ma. I tried to be with him but he doesn't wanna be together. Why won't he leave me alone?" She sat on the edge of the bed.

"Honey, he doesn't know how to make it right."

"Shooting out my tire and shattering my windshield definitely ain't the way." I pulled the covers over my body.

The day Zahra destroyed this room, Ms. Bell and Kalila used their own money to fix it up and made sure all the stuff was still here. They wanted me to come back, however; Zahra had to move in and there's no way we'd be able to co-exist in the same house after what happened.

Ms. Bell had a lock put on the door and made Zahra stay in the basement rooms. It didn't stop her from tryna get in my room. Kalila told me she caught her one day red handed tryna pick the lock. *Pathetic, I know.* I'm not sure what she thought she'd find but they let her ass have it.

Nevertheless; my son and I were more than comfortable in the new apartment. My mom even came over more, I guess because it's closer to where they stayed. She brought my stepfather and I almost slammed the door in his face. I had to remember him and my mother owned these so I had to at least be civil, especially; since I'm living rent free.

It's not that I hated him because I try never to hate anyone. I just feel like he took my mother away. He didn't want kids and sadly the woman he fell in love with had one and eventually; a grandchild. My mother was so in love with him, she pushed me right out the door. I blamed her for being stupid in love and him, for forcing her to do it.

The day he stopped by, he apologized for his actions. My mom cried and said she should've never been that blind to let her only child live with a man who was still a kid himself. I understood and forgave the two of them. Unfortunately; years have gone by and all we can do now is try and make up for lost time.

The crazy thing is, once my stepfather met Axel. he's been wrapped around his finger. I swear he now has everything at their place as far as games, clothes and whatever else he wanted. I can barely get my son to come home between them, Ms. Bell and Axel's mom. A few times I had to stay wherever he was just to spend time with him.

Ever since Zahra said that shit in the hospital, I think he's scared she will come hurt me. He hasn't said it but whenever I leave he gives me a tight hug and calls me all the time. When it's time for bed, I have to stay on the phone until he falls asleep, just for him to wake me up early in the morning to check on me. Now that's one bitch I plan on beating up every time I see her. Call me ratchet or ghetto all you want. She had no business saying those things to him.

"Can I talk to her for a minute?" Ms. Bell and I turned towards the door. Kruz leaned on the wall with his hands in his pockets.

"Umm sure."

"Don't leave me with him. He's a maniac."

"You'll be fine." She smiled and closed the door behind her. I rolled over and had my back to him.

"What the fuck?" I felt my body being drug to the end of the bed.

"You wanna play games, right?" I didn't say anything as he laid the gun on the dresser.

"I know exactly what you want." I folded my arms.

"And what's that?"

"This." He lifted me up fast, tossed me against the wall, squeezed my cheeks together and forced his tongue inside.

"Get off me." I tried pushing him away as he unbuckled his jeans, pulled my sweater dress over my head, slid my panties over and inserted himself inside.

"Fuck You Kruz." My nails we're digging in his shoulders.

"You are ma." I found myself popping up and down. It was wrong but it felt so damn good.

"Oh shit." My body shook as he extracted that first orgasm out.

"You missed this dick." He looked down and then back up at me.

"My shit is white Rhythm. Keep cumming for me."

"No. Put me downnnnnnnnnn." I bit down on his neck as another one rushed out.

"You don't want that."

"Kruz, we have to.-" I stopped talking when he lifted me on his shoulders and ate my pussy. I gripped the side of his head and bit down on my lip hard as hell when he got another one out.

"What are you doing to me?" He let me down, removed my panties, bent me over and fucked me so good, I had to bite down on the comforter to keep from screaming.

"Throw it back Rhythm." He yanked my hair, pumped harder and drilled deeper.

"Yea. Like that." Once he smacked me on the ass, I came even harder.

"You're gonna make me cum Rhythm." I finally got the strength to throw it back the way he liked.

"Oh shit ma. Oh fuckkkkk!" He held my waist tight and released inside me. I felt his fingertips digging in my ass as he continued emptying all his seeds.

"Shit. I haven't felt that good in weeks." We separated slowly and I could feel our juices running down my leg.

"Where's the bathroom?" I pointed to the small one in here. Ms. Bell had them add a half of bath in here because of my son. She didn't want him to have accidents and the hall bathroom is at the other end.

"You good?" He lifted my leg and washed my pussy. It's nothing new for us to take turns cleaning each other up but something was on his mind and I could tell.

"I'm fine but we can't be having sex and we're not together." He dried both of us off, pulled his clothes up and used some mouthwash on the sink. I changed into some sweats and sat on the bed staring at him, stare at me.

"Were you ever gonna tell me?"

"Tell you what?" I was confused as hell.

"Come here." I stood and moved over to where he was.

"It's ok. I understand."

"Understand what? Kruz, I have no idea what you're talking about."

"When are you supposed to marry him?"

"Marry who?"

"Axel. And don't deny it because your mother had no problem blasting it. She's actually excited." I laughed at him.

"Kruz."

"That shit ain't funny Rhythm. How you make me fall in love with you, just to marry another nigga?" He swung the

90

door open and stormed down the steps. Kalila had Sasha in her hands and Jamaica was on the phone.

"Y'all couldn't wait until later? Didn't nobody wanna hear all that moaning." I gave her the finger.

"What's wrong bro?"

"This bitch getting married."

"Bitch?"

"You heard me."

"Was I a bitch when you were moaning?"

"The pussy real good but it don't change the fact you about to walk down the aisle with another nigga." Kalila snapped her neck.

"Who the fuck you marrying?"

"From what my mother said, Axel."

"Axel?"

"That's what I said."

"Let him know I'm still gonna fuck you when I want." Since he wanted to be smart and talk shit, I went along with it.

"When I marry him ain't no other nigga fucking me."

"Oh, so you are marrying him?"

"If you say so, I guess I am. I'm gonna make sure I fuck him even better…" I jumped back when he came closer.

"Stop fucking with him Rhythm." Jamaica stood in front of him.

"Why should I? Whenever he gets mad, I'm all kinds of bitches and ho's. I mean why would I stop being one for him?"

"Let's go Kruz." Jamaica was pushing him out the door.

"Don't bring your ass back around tryna get some of this banging pussy." He charged me and I ran in the room. I locked the door and heard Kalila begging him not to mess up the house.

"I'ma catch you outside Rhythm and you better pray I'm in a good mood."

"Just go punk."

"Kalila you better let her know who she fucking with." I heard the door close and crept out the room.

"Why you keep messing with him?"

"He always starting and where her dirty ass mother?"

"My mom had to take her to the hospital and y'all start with each other." I waved her off and took Sasha. She was so cute and I loved her fat cheeks.

"You beat her ass sis."

"I'm gonna do it everytime I see her. Shit, Axel is scared to death to be around her. That shit makes me mad every time I think about it."

"I don't blame you."

"Was she that bad? I couldn't tell because your man pushed me away." She smiled and picked the phone up go order food.

"I take it you didn't mention my niece or nephew in your belly."

"Nope. He's too violent and I'm gonna let him think I'm getting married. Can you believe my mother told him that?"

"Yup because she hasn't been around."

"That's her fault."

"Rhythm you can't be mad. She didn't know." I laid Sasha on my chest and put my head back. How the hell did

Kruz and I go from not speaking, to fucking, to not speaking again? He is too damn bipolar for me. I need to stay away from him.

"Why the fuck you keep fucking with her?" Jamaica barked on the side of me. We stopped by because Kalila sent a text Rhythm was about to whoop Zahra's ass and the petty part of me wanted to see it. I didn't appreciate Rhythm doing it while my daughter was there but at least Kalila made sure she was outta harms way.

Zahra needed her ass beat for pulling the shit at the hospital. She had no business shouting out her sucking me off. Then I find out about her sleeping with my brother and it's no telling what other shit she's done.

I can't front though. Rhythm had my dick hard as hell in that fitted sweater dress she wore. It came in handy when I scooped her small ass up off the bed and fucked the shit outta her. My dick was happy as hell to be inside her and I don't care who knew it. Something about her, wouldn't allow me to stay away no matter what her mother said.

Hell yea, my feelings were hurt when she mentioned Rhythm getting married because in my head, she belonged to me. Then, she didn't deny marrying him which only meant,

I'm gonna have to kill this Axel dude and make it look accidental because he is lil man's father. Say what you want but Rhythm is mine and I'm damn sure stingy and territorial over my stuff.

"Man, that's her crazy ass."

"Nigga, both of y'all need to cut out all the bullshit and let motherfuckers know y'all together."

"Whatever." I waved him off and pulled up at the hotel his pops was staying at. Jamaica was supposed to see him after checking on Kalila the night those two did dumb shit at the motel but we went out and got fucked up. I didn't blame him for blacking on his girl and it's my intention to do the same with Rhythm.

"She's gonna be the one you put in that empty box tattoo."

"How you figure?" We walked in the hotel.

"Because you two can't stay away from each other, you already said the sex is the best you ever had and you told her it didn't matter if she were married because you still fucking her. Who the hell says some shit like that?"

"I am gonna keep fucking her." I shrugged my shoulders.

"Bro. You know she's not the ho type so unless you taking it, she ain't giving it."

"What the fuck ever." I ignored him but he's right. Rhythm isn't the type to sleep with multiple men, nor is she getting married. I'm gonna deal with the other shit after this meeting.

"Hey son. Kruz." His pops stepped to the side and let us in his suite. Some woman was there barely dressed and had the nerve to lick her lips at me and Jamaica. Right then we knew she wasn't his main.

"Beat it." Jamaica barked and she sat there.

"Bitch, you can't hear?" Jamaica lifted her by the hair and pushed her out the door. I tossed the purse, phone and few clothes to her just as it closed in her face.

"You rude as hell nigga."

"Says the motherfucker who shot out a chick's windshield and tires because she didn't wanna be around you."

"I bet she won't do it again." I smirked and laughed on the inside at how mad Rhythm was, which reminded me I had to send a text to Drew and get a tow truck there. We had someone who can have her shit fixed in no time.

"Did you read the papers?" I poured a shot from the bar listening to him and his father discuss his mom and her death. Afterwards, I dropped him off and headed to the strip club.

****

"You fucking that pole up." I told the stripper in front of me. I was still at the club tryna get drunk outta my mind. I couldn't even be comfortable with all the bitches tryna fuck.

"Damn." I watched her go into a split and crawl over to me. My dick was hard as hell.

"Can I go home with you daddy?" She was on my lap in a straddling position, kissing on my neck.

"No!" I heard and watched the chick's facial expression change as she was being drug off my lap by the hair.

"Not this shit again. Rhythm what the fuck?"

"Don't what the fuck me." She dared the stripper to say something and asked the security to escort her out the section.

98

"Shit, it's after one in the got damn morning. You think I wanna be here?"

"Then why are you?" I took a sip of my drink.

"Because my best friend and her man went outta town for the night. Your best friend." She pointed in my chest.

"Begged me to come see if you were ok. By the way, he owes me a thousand dollars for this." She stood there tapping her foot.

"That's y'all shit. You should've told him no."

"Whatever. Let's go." She stood there waiting for me to get up.

"I ain't going nowhere."

"Are you serious?"

"Yup. Now move so I can watch more strippers."

"Ughhhhh." She sat next to me on the small couch and rested her head on the side.

"What you doing yo?"

"In order to make my money, I have to make sure you get home safe. Therefore; I guess we'll be watching this scattered and stank pussy together. Matter of fact, wake me up

99

when you ready." I stared at her to see if she were joking. Once she snatched the jacket I came with off the other side of me, covered up her arms and rolled over, I knew she was.

"Yo, take yo ass home."

"You ready?"

"No."

"Then I'm not going nowhere." I felt her feet on my lap and shook my head. What in the hell type of shit she on?

"Let's go."

"Dammit. Make up your mind Kruz." She stood and threw my jacket at me.

I watched her from behind and grabbed my dick thinking about the last time I was inside her. Rhythm had a nice body and she knew I loved seeing her in leggings, which is exactly what she has on. Let's not forget the damn short shirt that barely covers her breasts so I can tell she didn't have a bra on either. If I didn't know any better, I'd say she came like this on purpose.

"Hey Kruz." I turned and saw the chick Rhythm beat up.

After the hospital incident, shorty wanted to fuck but my head wasn't in it. Yea, I promised to give her some if she didn't press charges but what I look like fucking a bitch with a black eye and crooked nose? Her body was in pain too. I know damn well she wouldn't have been able to take it. I've been avoiding her ever since.

"What up?" I saw Rhythm turn around and knew it would be some mess if I didn't make her leave.

"I thought..." She cut her sentence short.

"You thought what?" Rhythm smirked.

"Never mind." This bitch was scared to death of Rhythm.

"Look whatever your name is. Kruz and I are not together, therefore; don't feel bad for talking to him. I'm only here to make sure he gets home safe; per his friend."

"Oh."

"Hurry up Kruz. I'm going to sleep after I drop you off." She snatched my truck keys and walked off to give us privacy. Maybe she is over me because the old Rhythm wouldn't allow another chick to converse with me.

"Are you and I still gonna hook up or what?"

"That's up to you. I see you healed so I'm down."

"A'ight. Call me when you get home and I'll come through." I told her ok; knowing damn well it ain't happening.

"You good?" Rhythm questioned when I closed the door.

"Perfect." I grabbed her hand before she pulled off.

"If you drive stupid in my shit, I'ma fuck you up."

"Boy, don't nobody care about this stupid truck but you. Now move. Your breath smells like weed and a whole lotta liquor."

"So." She pulled off.

"So, it's making me sick." She rolled the window down.

"Unless you pregnant, why would it make you sick?" She sucked her teeth.

"Can you just be quiet?"

"I don't have to be quiet in my own shit." I could see how mad she was getting and laughed. We both knew how to press each other's buttons.

"What's the code?" She parked next to the gate and looked at me.

"I'll put it in."

"Hurry up Kruz. It's late."

"Stop all the whining." I stumbled out, pressed the buttons and waited for the gate to open.

"Ok. I'm safe." She stepped out the truck and told me to open the door. I walked on the side where she was and placed myself in front of her.

I placed a small kiss on her lips to see if she'd deny my advance and when she didn't, it was on. My hands slid up her legs and under her shirt. Just like I expected, no bra. I lifted it over her head, removed her sneakers, helped her out the pants and panties and sat her on the hood. I asked if it were too hot and she told me no.

I let my tongue run over my bottom lip, as both of my hands were now massaging her breasts. The moans were silent at the moment, which will change soon. I swirled my tongue over one of her nipples and let my hand continue caressing the other. I moved down to her belly button and watch as her head fell back the second two of my fingers thrusted inside.

"Oh shit Kruz." She began fucking my fingers and grinding on my face that's now in between those sexy thighs. Her clit was getting sensitive as the orgasm came closer.

"Fuckkkkkkk." I felt her body trembling as her juices shot out.

"Damn that pussy taste as good as it looks." I pulled her up by the arms and slid her from the car and onto my dick. I thrusted inside with one push.

I didn't go slow or attempt to make love. I wanted her to feel me all the way up to her chest if it's possible.

"Ahhhhhhh. Kruz."

"You got this ma." I could feel her hips pushing down on me to try and keep up.

"Hold on Rhythm." I carried her over to the house, placed her against the wall and continued giving her pussy a beating.

"Kruz." I put her down, moved back to the truck, put her hands on the hood and forced myself back in.

"Yea." My hand was wrapped around her throat. Her body was moving forward and the truck was moving too.

"I love you so much. Shittttt." Her hands were now gripping the bumper as I arched her back more.

"I love you too Rhythm and you're not marrying that nigga. You hear me?" Something made me snap and I started fucking her harder. The thought of another man touching her made me angry.

"Ok baby. Fuck. Fuck. Fuck." Her cream coated my dick. I fucked her in every position possible in the truck, my driveway, on the lawn and anywhere else we could.

"I'm about to cum Rhythm." We had been at it for so long, I couldn't hold it in.

"Go ahead baby." I gripped her ass while she rode me on the front porch.

"Shit." She moaned out and grabbed the side of the chair we were in. I grabbed her neck and forced my tongue in her mouth.

"Mmmmmmmm." Both of us let go and sat there breathing heavy.

"I'm pregnant." She whispered and a smile graced my face. I didn't even think to question the paternity because I've been nutting in her since day one. I'm not saying, I was tryna get her pregnant, but I didn't take precautions not to either.

"It's about time."

"What?" She lifted her head and looked at me.

"I did it on purpose." I stood with her in my arms. My soft dick slid out as I walked to where my jeans were on the lawn to grab my keys.

"Yup and if you think about getting rid of it, I'll keep your ass locked up and kill you after delivery."

"You're so violent." She bit down on my neck and started sucking on it.

"Only over you." I shut the door with my foot and took her upstairs. I'm tired as fuck.

I laid in bed with Kruz totally regretted what took place a few hours ago. I mean my body craved his touch and every bit of pleasure he bestowed on me, but the fact remain he still cheated, called me all types of bitches and ho's and stay threatening me.

Some women think it's cute when a man loves them to death but a bitch like me is nervous. What if he really kills me? I've heard the stories about him and his team. Plus, Kalila told me the guys at the motel work for them and I see how they get down.

I turned over and stared as he slept. I'm not gonna lie; I'm still madly in love with him. However; he's a savage and I'm a good girl most of the time. He and I are definitely compatible in many ways but he has to do better in order to keep me.

He thinks I don't know about the chick from the club supposedly coming over. See, Kruz has unlocked his phone in front of me many times and I've never felt the need to go behind his back and check until now. And it's only because it went off nonstop. As a woman who just slept with him, I feel it's my duty to see who it is.

When I opened it, the chick Natalie sent a few explicit messages, along with a few asking where he stayed and what time he wanted her to come over. I could be a bitch and respond but I also know he doesn't allow anyone here and would probably kill her if she approached his gate. I don't want anyone's death on my hands or conscience.

I eased out the bed slowly and covered him up. I hated to leave but again, I knew my worth.

I heard his phone go off again and my nosy ass went and checked it. This time it was Zahra begging him to see her. I laughed my ass off when she sent a picture of her in lingerie.

She's desperate as fuck and being the petty person I am. I lifted the covers up, laid down next to him, put his arm around my neck and snapped a picture with the deuces up. *Send*. I went to get up and the weight of his arm held me there.

"Did you snap a picture of your stomach for her too?"

"How you know what I'm doing?"

"You woke me up when you laid next to me." He tossed the phone on the floor and pulled me on top.

"Why your pussy getting wet?" I sucked my teeth as he continued rubbing my clit.

"Sssssss."

"Ride me." I didn't get a chance to protest because he lifted me up and slammed my body down. His girth is nothing to fuck with and it's always painful in the beginning.

I threw my head back as he moved my hips in circles. Kruz had a way of making the sex explosive and different every time. Like now, he had me leaning half way off the bed with one leg on his shoulder and the other flat on the bed. It sounds crazy so imagine how it looks. The amount of pleasure he gave always outweighed the minor pain.

"Your sexy ass about to have my baby." He moved in circles, stretching me wider.

"I'm cumming Kruzzzzzzz. Oh Godddddd." I came so hard he had to lift me up and stop me from shaking. I don't think I've ever experienced one this strong in my life.

"Go break it off with that nigga today." He threw me on his shoulder and smacked my ass on the way in the bathroom.

"Kruz, us having sex doesn't make us a couple."

"Rhythm you been mine."

"I'd agree if you didn't cheat on me." He put the soap down, slid his hand through my hair and brought my face close to his.

"I'm sorry Rhythm and it will never happen again." The kiss had me wet again.

"I don't know about that. What if y'all are alone and your feelings resurface and..."

"Not gonna happen because you're the only woman I want."

"Maybe we should take a break. See if this is what we really want."

"You had one already. Ain't no more breaks Rhythm." He said it with finality as he let my hair go and started washing up.

"The way I see it is, you got even."

"How is that?" I folded my arms and washed him scrub his body.

"You left me, beat up my ex and I let you punch me a few times. Had it been anyone else laying hands on me, they'd be six feet under."

"You always threatening somebody." He moved my hands and started washing me up.

"I only make promises."

"You promised not to cheat." He ignored me, finished washing my body and stepped out.

"Oh, you don't have anything to say?" I walked in the room dripping wet.

"Nope." He slid his legs in the boxers.

"Why not?"

"Because it's over and I'm not dwelling on it."

"Fine. I'm outta here." I moved past and he grabbed my wrist.

"I know you wanna make me pay for cheating and believe me when I tell you I did." I rolled my eyes.

"I was fucked up after hearing you were at the motel and something may have happened to you. I had my boy speed to the hospital just so I could see you were ok and that's when your mother blurted out this marriage shit."

"Kruz?" He shushed me with his index finger.

"I was pissed but still had trouble sleeping knowing you were hurt over the motel shit and the Zahra crap."

"I'm not getting married."

"Then why did your mother say it?"

"We're not tight Kruz." I explained our situation and I must say the smile gracing his face after hearing I wasn't getting married made my heart melt. He really did love me and wanted me all to himself.

"Now that all the BS is over, this back and forth with us is for kids Rhythm. Either we're gonna do this or not?" He stood in front of me and lifted my face.

"I'm not saying you're not hurt and you have every reason to be guarded but I'm not gonna be around a woman who isn't sure what she wants."

"I want nothing more than to be with you but..."

"Stop focusing on the past and what may happen in the future Rhythm. Let's focus on the present, the right now." He pecked my lips.

"I love you and you're gonna have my child. All I have is my word and if you want us, you're gonna need to trust me again."

"How?"

"I don't know." I sat on the bed watching him get dressed. He turned to me and smiled. What is it about him that makes me melt?

"There's only one way to make you trust me."

"And that is?"

"Get dressed and I'll show you." I did like he asked and prayed whatever it is would help because as bad as I want him, the trust had to be restored or this relationship is doomed from the start.

****

"Mommy!" Axel ran straight to me when I picked him up from his father's place. I haven't seen him in a few days.

"How are you sweetie. I missed you so much." I squeezed him hard and kissed all over his face.

"Caroline made me a big chocolate cake and daddy let me eat a bowl of ice cream." His arms were around my neck.

"Wow! Did you get a belly ache?'

"Yea and I was on the toilet a lot."

"Yuk." I pinched my nose and he laughed.

"What up?" His father walked out looking sexy as hell. You could tell he had a fresh haircut and the clothes looked brand new. But then again, he barley ever wore anything more than once. He's been the same since high school. I guess he would being his father now had quite a bit of dealerships.

"Not much. Thanks for keeping him."

"Rhythm, don't disrespect me."

"What?"

"You don't ever need to thank me for keeping my son. He is always welcomed to stay as long as he wants."

"I know but you have another family over here."

"He's my family too and regardless if we're together, so are you." He moved the strands of hair out my face. I cleared my throat and moved away.

"You're the one who got away Rhythm and I still regret it to this day, but I'm glad you're happy."

"I am." I smiled putting Axel in the backseat.

"Is he good to you?" I closed the door and blew my breath.

"He's very good to me but like most men, they slip up and he did."

"Can't be because of the sex, that's for damn sure." He licked his lips and I smacked him on the side of the arm.

"He had recently got outta a relationship and fell victim to his ex. You know the same as you with me, in the beginning of you and her."

When he first started dating Caroline, him and I crept around for a minute. I know it wasn't right and I probably would've continued but once he gave me a disease, that was it. I think it taught him a lesson too because as far as I know, he doesn't cheat, or as much and if he does, he uses two rubbers, let him tell it.

"Shit, I'll still fall victim to that good pussy and head."

"Bye Axel." I laughed walking over to the driver's side.

"Anyway, tell Caroline thank you for making him a cake and he'll be here for the fitting." I referred to his wedding taken place in a few weeks. My mother was correct about him getting married, it just wasn't to me.

"Don't worry about it. I took him already."

"Oh ok. Does he need anything?" He gave me a look.

"I now you're his father but I'm his mother and I want to make sure he knows both of his parents are taken care of him." He walked over to me.

"Rhythm, I know you're doing the best you can under the circumstances. What I don't understand is why you're refusing to use any of the money in the bank?" I had thousands in the bank under my son's name but it was child support.

"Because its money for him and he doesn't need anything."

"You're his mother and if he lives with you, then it's yours. Rhythm look how big this house is." He waved his arm.

"There's no reason my son doesn't live the same." He's right. I have the means to live lavish but felt like the child support is supposed to be used on him and since he didn't want for nothing, I left it in the bank. No one knows about it, not even Kalila. It's not a secret. I just don't think it's necessary to mention it.

"He will Axel."

"When?"

"Right now. We're going to our new place."

"With that nigga?"

"Yup." Kruz asked me to move in with him and I agreed. At first, I wasn't hesitant but he made me an offer I couldn't refuse.

"I wanna meet him at some point Rhythm." I sat in my car that Kruz brought me. My car was fixed but since he was trying to get back in my good graces I made him buy me a brand new Jaguar and its nice as hell. Top of the line everything in it too.

"I agree. You two should meet, especially; since he's gonna be in my life for a long time."

"Do I know him?"

"I'm not sure. His name is Kruz Garcia and…"

"SAY WHAT?" He shouted and I smirked.

"Exactly! I don't have to say a word for you to know we'll be well taken care of."

"Rhythm he's dangerous and I'm not sure it's a good idea for my son to…" I put my hand up, got back out the car and closed the door.

"Axel, I never bothered you about your choice and I expect the same in return." He blew his breath.

"He's dangerous in the streets but not with me and he loves Axel." He turned his head and I made him face me.

"We both know I won't allow anything to happen to our son."

"I know but.-"

"It's time to let someone love me Axel. I'm tired of being alone."

"I get that but why him?"

118

"Actually, I don't have a choice." I laughed to myself.

"Why is that? Is he holding you against your will or something? I may not be able to beat him up but I'll help you leave the state."

"No fool."

"Then why can't you leave?" I put my mouth close to his ear.

"Because he had this banging ass pussy and head. He ain't tryna let another nigga smell the soap I wash in." I kissed his cheek, got in the car and pulled off with him standing there stuck. It's his loss.

"Where we going mommy?" I glanced in the rearview mirror at my son staring out the window. I loved him with every breath in my body and would die for him and the one in my stomach.

"To our new house."

"We got a new house? Is it big? Do I have a game system?" He bombarded me with questions until we pulled up.

"This is Mr. Kruz house."

"Now it's ours."

"REALLY!" He got excited, unbuckled himself and jumped out. Once the door opened and Kruz came out, he ran over and started asking for his room and stuff. I walked in the house and closed the door behind me.

"WOW! This is big." I heard Axel yelling from upstairs. A few minutes later I felt hands around my waist.

"How did his father take it?" He placed a kiss on my neck.

"Fine, He wants to meet you and I think it's a good idea." I turned and put my arms around his neck.

"A'ight. Let me know when."

"That was easy." He lifted me in his arms and sat me on the counter.

"He's his father and I'd feel the same about my son. I mean if Zahra ever meets a new nigga, he can't come around unless I do a full background check." I stared at him.

"But then again, she'll be dead soon so it won't matter because you'll be her mother and you ain't going nowhere."

"Kruz."

"I don't wanna hear it Rhythm. I told her if I found out she fucked my brother, I was gonna kill her."

"Yea but…" I jumped off the counter when he backed away.

"But nothing. Get to cooking. Me and my stepson hungry." He smacked me on the ass and left me standing there with my mouth hanging open. I may not care for Zahra and will probably whoop her ass a few more times but I don't think he should kill her.

"So what's the problem?" I asked Rhythm. She came over to tell me about Kruz wanting to kill Zahra. I don't see what the issue is.

"Kalila, you can't be ok with him killing her." I stopped frying the chicken and looked at her.

"Rhythm, Zahra is a bitch and of course, I wouldn't wish death on her but you mean to tell me in four years, she didn't know the type of nigga Kruz was?"

"I'm sure she did but…"

"But nothing sis. Look." I took a seat on the bar stool next to her.

"Zahra knows the type pf man Kruz is and thought his love would stop him from killing her. What she didn't realize is he ain't the type of nigga who's gonna let someone play him."

"I guess."

"My sister made her bed and now she has to lay in it." I shrugged and went back to the stove to check on the food.

"What about Sasha?" I turned the chicken over.

"What about her? Her mother will be dead." I put the fork down and wiped my hands on the apron.

"KALILA!"

"Shit, she will be. Plus, her new mom is going to take very good care of her and me and my mom will be around. Oh yea, so will his family."

"Why do I bother talking to you sometimes?"

"Because you love me." I cheesed real hard.

"I think he should let Sasha growing up knowing her mother."

"Let's be clear Rhythm." I folded my arms.

"Sasha will know who her real mother is and I may feel a little remorse for my sister but not enough to have her back. Did you not forget she almost let my mother lose the house? She didn't give a fuck about her going homeless because she's selfish. Let's not forget the shit she yelled out to Axel in the hospital room. And last but not least, not only was she fucking Kruz brother but she basically turned his mom against him, over you." I walked over to where she was.

"Rhythm, no one deserves to die but when you play with fire you get burned."

"Yea. You're right."

"I know. Now stop with the whining and tell me how it is living in that big ass house."

"Besides my pussy being sore almost every night, its good."

"Bitch, you got live in dick now. You better appreciate that shit because once you deliver its gonna be a while before you get more." She gave me the finger and started telling me how Kash has been spending more time over there. He is even doing better in school and as of lately, no one has called to say he stole anything. I believe it has everything to do with Kruz. He scared to death of him.

"Ok now tell me why you won't move in with Jamaica." I waved her off.

"I'm serious Kalila. You and him been together almost three years now. Shit, you should've moved in with him way before I moved in with Kruz. What's the holdup?" I put the last batch of chicken on the paper towel in the strainer to drain the excess grease.

"He hasn't asked me."

"WHAT?"

"He hasn't asked and I'm not pressuring him to."

"You're five months pregnant and living with your mom. What's his problem?"

"I think he hasn't asked because of the shit with the Kandy bitch."

"What you mean?"

"I hear him on the phone at night."

"With another bitch. Oh hell no."

"No fool. I think he learned his lesson from doing that shit."

"Ok." We slapped hands.

"He don't wanna sleep alone again." We both busted out laughing.

"Anyway, I heard him saying something about his father wants her dead and she's the cause of someone taking from their trap house. Whatever she has going on in her life, is affecting his and I don't think he wants me involved."

"Too late. The bitch knows who you are."

"That's what I was thinking but he doesn't involve me in shit. The only way I'm gonna find out is if you ask your man."

"HELL FUCKING NO!"

"Come on sis."

"No Kalila. The last time I followed your stupid ass plan, I ended up in the hospital and had to go through hoops to get my man back."

"That's your mom's fault for opening her mouth."

"What about this?" She pointed to the small scar on her forehead.

"You always focus on the past."

"Bitch, really?"

"I'm just saying. All I want is for you to ask. Do it while y'all fucking."

"First off, when we fucking, you or no one else is on my mind."

"I'm talking about when y'all done."

"Bye." She stood to leave an sat when my mother came in looking stressed. Her facial expression had Zahra all over it and I hated to ask what happened.

"Your sister got me written up today."

"How the hell she do that?" My mother took a seat and let her head drop back.

"I wasn't answering her calls because every phone call is her wishing death on Rhythm and why don't I love her the same. Blah, blah, blah." I gave Rhythm a look that said she better let Kruz kill her.

"Anyway, the secretary let her in because she threatened to fight her if she didn't."

"Zahra can't even fight."

"I know Kalila but my secretary white so she doesn't know." Me and Rhythm laughed.

"Long story short, she comes in my office screaming like a damn maniac about me not answering her calls and neglecting my granddaughter. Security comes in and she starts acting worse. I mean you would think she belongs on the crazy floor in the hospital."

"What the hell is wrong with her?" Rhythm asked with her face turned up.

"My boss came in and told me she had no choice but to write up an incident report. Kalila, I've been at my job for over twenty years and have never in my life been written up. In one day, your sister managed to get me written up and put on one day suspension."

"WHAT?" I was pissed because my mom is the sweetest person and her job loved her. For my sister to act like that only fueled the fire in me towards her.

"I'm gonna whoop her ass."

"Kalila, leave it alone. I don't need her returning because you went after her."

"Ma, she can't keep getting away with hurting you." I grabbed my keys and ended up grabbing my stomach. The pain was so bad, I asked them to hurry and get me to the hospital.

****

"You good ma? What the fuck happened?" Jamaica rushed in with Kruz and the guy Drew, who I met a while back.

"I'm fine."

"This don't look fine." He pointed to the monitors on my arm, stomach and chest.

"Zahra did some shit."

"What? She put her hands on you?" He's definitely overprotective of me.

"No. not like that. Calm down Kenron." He sucked his teeth. He hated for me to call him that in public. Kruz and Drew started laughing.

"She almost got my mother fired from work and I was gonna fight her."

"Hold the fuck up. You were gonna what?" I covered my mouth.

"Don't hold it on now. Kalila, I swear if you lose my baby or die, I'm gonna kill you."

"How are you gonna kill me if I'm dead?"

"I'll die with you and kill yo ass again."

"Whatever." He pecked my lips and sat on the side of the bed asking me a million questions about the baby.

"Hey boo. You good?" Sabrina asked when she stepped in looking like a damn video vixen. All three men stared hard as hell at her. I guess they would with the tight ass jumpsuit and heels. One thing I can say about her, is she never left the house looking less than fabulous.

"Kruz, I will fuck you up in here if you don't stop staring at her." Rhythm barked.

"What? She sexy but not as sexy as you."

"And so is that male nurse walking the halls. Let me go see if I can stare at hm." She stood and he did the same.

"I wish the fuck you would."

"You better watch your fucking eyes."

"A'ight damn."

"Ummmm ok." Sabrina was uncomfortable as hell.

"Girl, it ain't you at all." Rhythm told her and dared Kruz to look at Sabrina again.

"This y'all friend?"

WHAP! I smacked the hell outta Jamaica's head when he gave her a once over.

"Yo! I'm about to." I folded my arms across my chest.

"You about to what?" He didn't say anything.

"Well, my girl ain't here and I'm gonna look. You sexy as fuck yo! And you wearing the shit out that outfit." Drew made everyone in the room laugh. It damn sure broke the tension.

"Anyway, what's up? I thought you were out of town with your new boo." Rhythm and I became close with her after we took the dance class with Dexter. She'd never be as close as me and my bestie but we were tight. We also knew she was with Kommon and refused to mention his name.

"We came back today because he had a doctor's appointment and I wanted to make sure you were good." Kruz fucked him up really bad. She felt bad but not as much because she told us about the time at the restaurant with my sister acting like a fucking fool. She told him then to tell his brother then and Kommon didn't listen.

"Oh ok. Well I'm glad you came but from now on, you'll have to wear some loose-fitting sweats and shirt around these perverts."

"I ain't no got damn pervert." Jamaica barked and put his face in my neck.

"I apologize. You know I would never try and entice your men."

"We know girl."

"Can I talk to you ladies in private?"

"Sure." I asked the guys to give us a minute and waited for them to leave. She sat on the bed next to me.

"Kommon wanted me to come ask Rhythm if she could get Kruz to sit down with him so he can explain what went down with him and Zahra."

"Are y'all tryna get me killed? First Kalila, now you. I swear you bitches really have no love for me."

"Dramatic as usual."

"Dramatic. Heffa, I'll show you dramatic. Watch this." She sat on the chair and put her legs out.

"KRUZ!" He came running in.

"What's wrong?" He immediately looked at Sabrina who had her hands up to say not her.

"I wanna fuck." The smirk on his face told me she did this shit a lot.

"Tell your friends goodbye."

"Give me a second." He told her to hurry up because now he's ready.

"Bitch, all you did is show you're a horny pervert like him. Now back to what Sabrina asked."

"Fuck you. How the hell you think I'm gonna get him to speak to Kommon?" She winked at Sabrina and I popped up.

"Nah, ahh bitch. I told you to fuck him and ask about Jamaica and you said.-"

"Bitch, I know what I said and I still ain't doing it because you need to ask him." She gave me the finger and told Sabrina she'd try and set it up but she wasn't making promises.

After we talked a little longer, the guys came in and the doctor discharged me. I hopped in the car with Jamaica and went to his house. I told him to rent a movie or something and I'll be right down.

133

"YOOOOOOO!" Jamaica had the biggest smile on his face when I came down the steps and called his name.

I stood there in some black fishnet stockings, a new bra set I got, just because and my hair was down the way he liked it. I kept it up because it made the back of my neck hot.

"You like?"

"Hell fucking yea, I like. Fuck that. I love this." He kissed my stomach and then my lips.

"I figured you were turned on by Sabrina, so it's only fair to give you your own fantasy."

"Correction ma." He lifted my face to his.

"She is a bad bitch, but she ain't got shit on you." He placed a kiss on my neck.

"You sure because…" I unbuckled his jeans and slid them and his boxers down.

"I'm positive K. Your pussy is the only one my dick wakes up for. I mean you can have a scarf on with different color clothes and bad breath and my man will still want you. Kalila Bell you are the only woman I see." I let him kiss the tears away that fell listening to him talk.

"Then why won't you ask me to live here with you?" He stepped away and stared at me.

"Kalila, I want you to wake up with me everyday but it's so much shit going on."

"I'm over here all the time though. I have the keys to every place you have. I do, right?" I asked thinking about Kruz giving Rhythm all his shit and not my sister who he was with longer.

"Ma, you have the keys to everything I own in this state and others. K, your name is on my fucking chest in big letters." I kissed each letter and played with his balls before squatting down.

"Then why don't I live here?" I placed the tip in my mouth and twirled it around.

"If you wanna stay with me, it can't be in this house. Oh fuckkkkk!" He grabbed my hair and made love to my face slow.

"Shitttttt. I'm selling this one." I went faster and jerked him quicker.

"Got damn ma." I sucked harder and smiled when he came. I got so nasty with it the next set of words out his mouth surprised me.

"Marry me." I used my hand to wipe my mouth and he helped me stand.

"Are you serious?" He leaned down and picked his jeans up.

"I was picking this up when Rhythm called and said you were at the hospital." He placed a humongous diamond on my finger.

"Jamaica, this is huge. You didn't have to buy.-" He shushed me with his lips, carried me up the steps and made love to me until I couldn't take it. I's about to be a married woman.

"So, you popped the question huh?" I turned to see Blue standing there in a black catsuit. Her body was on full display and I had to distance myself from her. Not because I wanted to fuck but because she's messy as hell and I can see her starting some shit between me and Kalila.

The night I called her and Kalila caught me, I went over the next day and gave her a goodbye fuck. Granted, we went all day but when I left, it was made clear for her to stay away. I'm not gonna say I don't miss fucking different bitches but if it meant losing the best thing in my life, then it's not worth it.

Right now, she's bending over in front of me to pick a napkin up off the floor to get my attention. I can admit she's making it hard but I ain't no weak nigga. I shook my head at how thirsty she was being. Is this what women have stooped to?

Kruz thought it was a good idea to have drinks as an engagement party. I'm always down to get fucked up and since Kalila was with Rhythm going over wedding dresses, and ordering stuff for the baby at the other house, I may as well get out.

After she and I fucked the hell outta each other the night I proposed, she's been with me ever since. I've always wanted her to stay with me but with Kandy out there plotting with her new man, I didn't wanna bring any extra attention to her. However; when Kalila asked why I didn't have her with me, I felt bad and gave in only because I did have another spot Kandy knew nothing about, or I hope she didn't.

The house we're staying in is closer to the new job she was hired for. Right now, they're letting her work from home due to the pregnancy. Six weeks after she delivers, they want her in the office.

I told her not to worry about working but she's not tryna hear it. Shit, Kruz told me Rhythm signed up for online college courses and she goes to the community college one night a week. We definitely ended up with two good girls. Hood chicks are ok but sometimes they don't know how to turn it off and who wants to be bothered with that each time you step out?

"Yup and you doing all this ain't gonna get me in bed." She smirked and moved in closer.

"No but this may." She put her tongue in my ear and attempted to slide her hands down my jeans.

"Bitch, are you crazy?" I mushed her in the head and watched her fall over the chair and on the floor. I look up and Sabrina was standing there with her arms folded and a snarl on her face. I ran my hand over my head and stared as she typed away on her phone. I knew she was texting Kalila and didn't even bother asking her not to.

It's funny how they met her a while ago and now she is as tight with them as Kalila and Rhythm. The second my phone rang, I picked it up without looking.

"It's time for you to come home."

"K, it's not even one yet."

"Kenron, you got twenty minutes to get here or I promise my fat ass will walk in that bitch and cause a fucking scene."

"A'ight yo." I hung up and looked at Sabrina pretending to clean her nails.

"You do know I wasn't gonna fuck her." She walked with me outside the club.

"Listen Jamaica." She peeped her surroundings before talking.

"Blue is my cousin through marriage only and I know for a fact she's tryna trap you."

"What you say?"

"I didn't know who you were when she first started telling me about you."

"When was this?"

"About two months ago. She only mentioned you because of who I'm with."

"And who are you with?" I could see her struggling to tell me.

"Kommon."

"Kommon who? The only one I know is.-" I stopped.

"No wonder the girls are close with you."

"That's not it. We were cool before I even met him."

"Oh shit. Kruz, is gonna have a ball with this shit."

"Whatever." She waved her hand.

"Anyway, Blue has been tryna get you to come over so she can drug and fuck you with no condom."

"Say word."

"Word. Let me go. I'm up next."

"You strip?" I looked her up and down.

"I used to. Kommon don't play that shit." Kommon may not have been around us a lot but he always said he didn't want a stripper for a girlfriend. Hell, we all said that growing up.

"I'm up next because if you haven't noticed, I'm the VJ introducing the strippers." I never paid attention to the person who did it. She went to walk in and I grabbed her arm.

"What you text my girl?" She smirked.

"Jamaica, I know you find women attractive like most men but please stop making it obvious."

"What you mean?"

"Kalila feels like now that she's pregnant your attention is no longer focused on her. She thinks you're gonna cheat on her."

"I'm good. Ain't no woman out here comparing to her, no matter how she looks on the outside." I said in a way letting her know, she may have a bad body but she still ain't got shit on my girl.

"Tell her that. Let her know she's still the best-looking woman in your eyes. Jamaica, women become very self-conscious during pregnancy. Especially; when they know how women are throwing themselves at men these days. Speak of the devil." She pointed to Blue coming out the door and headed in our direction.

"I'm out."

"JAMAICA!"

"Let's go Blue." Sabrina pulled her inside and I'm glad she did because I didn't feel like smacking bitches tonight. I drove home and blew my breath in the air as I stepped out the car. I knew my girl was about to go off.

"Soooooo I'm not good enough? You had to go see some strippers and let them touch on you?" I dropped my keys on the table and walked over to her.

"Don't touch me with that bitch on you." I hated to see her angry because then she'd curse. Kalila has class and it's one of the reasons I fell for her.

"Fine. Let me shower."

"Why? You fucked her in the parking lot or something?"

"K, you bugging."

"Am I?" She stood and I smiled at her stomach. I'm excited as hell to be a father and everyday she gets more and more beautiful to me.

"K, stop letting these bitches make you think I want them."

"You allowing them to touch you so why not?"

"The second she touched me, I pushed her off."

"I saw the video.

"Video?"

"Yea. I saw when she approached you. But my problem isn't with you pushing her. My problem is with you even allowing her to be that close."

"I didn't know she was gonna do that."

"Which is the exact reason you should've beat your feet the minute you saw her."

"You right." I didn't wanna argue all night so I just agreed.

"See Kenron bitches know when they spot a man without his woman, all they have to do is talk nasty and most men are down. I give it to you for handling it but again, the bitch should've never even been comfortable in your presence."

"What's that supposed to mean?"

"It means let a bitch know the first time what it is and she won't even attempt to try you."

"K, she knows I'm engaged."

"But do you?" She stormed off and into one of the downstairs bedrooms.

I went to shower, put on my pajamas and strolled in the room with her. She was laying on her side watching television. I moved close and hugged her.

"I fucked up Kalila and I'm sorry. You're right. She should've never been close or even comfortable enough to

approach me. If you felt like I disrespected you, I apologize."
She turned over and wiped her eyes.

"Why you crying?"

"You sure you're ready for marriage? If not, we can
Co-parent." I quieted her down with my lips and took her body
to ecstasy. I loved the hell outta Kalila and I'm gonna make
sure Blue never approaches me again.

****

I woke up the next day on a mission. Kalila was still
asleep so I eased out the bed and handled my hygiene. I sent
the text to Drew asking if the motel was empty. Once he told
me yes, I sent another one out to Blue. I wanted her to meet me
there and within seconds she responded.

I placed my phone on the clip, snatched my keys and
sped over to the motel. I'll be damned if Rhythm's car wasn't
in a parking spot. Kruz hated her working but like her friend,
she too refused to stay in the house.

I used the key to get in and was happy to see it cleaned.
Ever since the shit went down with the girls, we had to be on

point. The entire room had to be gutted because dudes' brains were all over the walls.

I sent a guy in to check for fingerprints and Kalila's were everywhere. She's so got damn nosy, she even had some on the damn zip ties. It's funny because I could picture her picking stuff up tryna figure out what it's used for. I blame the clean-up people too because it should've been no trace of anything there.

Anyway, the walls had to come down, along with the rug needing to be changed. When the guys do a hit, the place is covered with tarp and sheets we burn later. Unfortunately, my girl was messy as hell and DNA, blood and whatever else could link the murder to her was there.

"Hey baby." Is the first thing she said when the door opened. I moved to the side and allowed her access.

"HELL FUCKING NO NIGGA!" Blue turned around when Rhythm yelled. I pushed her back and shut the door behind me.

"Take your pregnant ass in the office."

"I'm telling my girl."

"Telling her what Rhythm." I folded my arms across my chest.

"How you here with another bitch and she home pregnant?" I gripped her arm, walked down a few doors and then in the parking lot. I picked my phone up and made a call.

"What up? You done?" Kruz spoke in the phone and she rolled her eyes.

"Nah bro. I ain't did shit yet because your blocking ass woman here."

"Why the hell she there?"

"I don't know. Ask her. Here." I handed Rhythm the phone and walked her to the office.

"Do not come out." She gave me the finger. I walked down and back in the room to find Blue was spread eagle and naked.

"I see you ready."

"Always for you baby."

"I can't tell." She came over and squatted down in front of me. She knew I always wanted my dick sucked first.

I lifted her face as she attempted to unbuckled my jeans.

147

"My fiancé found out you tried to fuck."

"Who cares?" I smirked.

"I do."

SNAP! I broke her neck and watched her body hit the ground. The door opened with Drew and two guys to clean the mess.

"Damn, she was bad. You should've let me fuck first." One of the guys said and I left the room shaking my head. I saw Rhythm coming in my direction.

"Next time can you.-" She glanced the parking lot.

"Can you commit a crime on my day off." She whispered and passed me the phone.

"If you stop being nosy, you would've never known."

"I'm always gonna be nosy when my future brother in law is with another chick. I don't care if you get mad either." She shrugged her shoulders and dipped off into the office. I called my boy when I sat in the car.

"Bro, we have the nosiest females I've ever met in my life." Kruz busted out laughing.

"True. What's up with tonight? Y'all still stopping by?"
We we're having movie night at their crib. We tried to do
something with the girls once a week to keep them happy.

"Yea. I'll pick up the liquor."

"A'ight, I got the trees." I disconnected the call and
drove to see my pops. We got a lotta shot going on right now
and I'm making sure everything is secure before moving
forward. I don't need no fuck ups.

"Don't be having my daughter around that bitch either." I told Kruz as he put Sasha in her car seat. He turned around, stood there and his stare sent chills down my spine.

I moved away and asked why didn't he come in to get Sasha. He refused to step foot in my condo and I always had to bring her out.

The results came in the mail a week and a half after taking a new test and a bitch was nervous and scared to open the envelope. I even closed my eyes because I was afraid the baby would be Kommon's.

I know most people thought it was his but truth be told, we may have had a few slip ups but we always used protection. He did say the condom came off a few times and yes, I was worried until the due date was announced. Kommon and I had just started messing around and weren't having sex as much.

When Kruz told me, he was ready for kids I immediately stopped taking the pills just like I told him. I also knew it would take a while before I'd get pregnant because I had been on them for years. We'd have sex all the time and in weird places just to try and get me pregnant faster.

A few months before Kruz busted me cheating, Kommon and I were on a break. He didn't know about his brother but he knew it was someone and voiced his anger about being a side nigga. He stopped speaking to me and even blocked me. I didn't care and started sexing Kruz even more; sore pussy and all.

Low and behold, Kommon and I ran into one another and we picked up where we left off. He still voiced his concern and even asked me to leave the dude. I refused and the last day we were together, he left the hotel mad.

I felt extremely sick that day and it had been going on for weeks. I never told anyone, called my mother and she asked if I were expecting. When I told her I'm not sure, she told me to get a test and sure enough those pink lines popped up.

Excited as hell, I rushed home to tell Kruz. Unfortunately; he was on his way out and instead of waiting for him to return like I always did, I threw a tantrum and my secret slid out; literally.

I never intended on him finding out who the person was but once Kommon knew it was his brother; he couldn't hold it in. He felt bad and even told me Kruz would probably kill him or try. I asked why he thought that and he told me, *Kruz said he couldn't wait for him to meet his girl because she was the best thing in his life, and he couldn't wait to make her his wife.* I felt like shit and it wasn't anything I could do to erase the past or have his brother keep it a secret at this point. When it came out in the hospital room, I knew he was gonna kill me which is exactly why I held my daughter tight.

"Shut the fuck up yo." He strapped her in the back and closed the door.

"I'm serious Kruz. I'm her mother and..." He cut me off.

"Not for long."

"What?" He turned to face me.

"Oh, you thought I was joking when I said I'm gonna kill you if I found out you fucked my brother."

"Kruz." I placed my hand on his arm.

"Bitch, I will break your fucking wrist." He had a firm grip and twisted it behind my back.

"You're hurting me." He tossed me against his truck and my face hit the window.

"Rhythm is in my life and will be forever. Sasha will definitely be around her." He mushed me in the head and yanked me away from his truck.

"How could you hurt the woman who birthed your child?" I rubbed my wrist.

"You ain't no fucking woman." The look he gave made me feel embarrassed for some reason.

"Let me show you something." He came back to where I stood, removed his shirt and pointed to the fresh tattoo on his chest. I covered my mouth staring at Rhythm's name in the box I swore would only hold mine.

"You got one time to try something with her and your demise will come sooner than later."

"You're really gonna kill me?" I wiped the tears falling down my face as he put his shirt on.

"Hell motherfucking yea. The only reason you're not dead yet is because I love seeing the fear on your face. Plus, I don't know how I'm gonna do it yet." He put his index finger under his chin like he was thinking.

"I want you to hurt and actually feel the pain. It may not be the same as what I felt hearing you cheated, and with my brother but it's close enough." He sat in his truck, and pulled on the side of me.

"You're so jealous of Rhythm that it's sickening. I mean what type of bitch has that kinda time on her hands?"

"She ain't nothing to be jealous of."

"Sure, she is. It's the exact reason you never let me meet your family. You knew deep down inside she'd catch my attention but the sad part is, is that even tho bitches may have sucked me off here and there, you were the only woman I ever wanted. The woman, I planned on waking up to for the rest of my life. The woman who was supposed to give me all my kids and ride off in the sunset with."

"Kruz, you know I still love you."

"I can honestly say, I'm over you Zahra and another woman has my heart." I rolled my eyes.

"She's what I've been missing and had you not fucked up she would've met someone else and I would've missed out."

"You haven't even known her that long." He smirked.

"It's almost a year and by the time she delivers, it'll be damn near two. Plus no one has a time limit on when they fall in love." He put up his two fingers and sped off. *Did he just say she's pregnant?*

****

"Ma, that's supposed to be my name on his chest. I'm the only one who's supposed to have his kids." I followed behind my mother in the kitchen. I brought Sasha over to see her and couldn't help but to discuss the shit with Kruz from the other night.

I thought about showing up at her job again but decided against it. My mother loved where she worked and the look on her face when the supervisor questioned what was going on,

155

made me feel bad. She's been at the job for years and I've barely ever been there so for me to show up, and show out put her in a bad place. It's her fault though because she should've answered my calls.

"Zahra, it's obvious he doesn't want you. Why can't you move on and find someone else?" She started washing dishes.

"Then he has my daughter with that bitch." I heard her slamming the dishes.

"What?" She tossed the dish rag in the sink and looked at me.

"That bitch as you call her, stepped up and moved in to help me pay for the mortgage. Something my own biological daughter wouldn't do."

"I told you to sell this piece of crap."

"If I did, where would you have stayed when he put you out?" She folded her arms across her chest.

"I could've gotten a room."

"But you didn't because you like to leech off everyone else."

"I do not."

"Yes you do and the only reason you're mad at Rhythm and Kruz's relationship is because he's no longer funding your outrageous lifestyle. You don't want her having anything."

"She has a baby daddy to help her."

"But Kruz is her man now. Therefore; he's gonna do everything for her. The same as he used to do for you, but it does appear that he's doing a lot more for her. She must be screwing him better. Oooops." My mother used her hand to cover her mouth and laugh. Is she really being petty?

"She won't be screwing him too long because I'm gonna make sure of it." I whispered on my way out.

"Whatever you're thinking about doing, I'd re think it."

"What?"

"I heard you talking shit. If you think Rhythm beat yo ass before, imagine what she'll do the next time and Kruz ain't about to let you do anything to her." I couldn't believe my mother was taken up for her.

"Ummm, whose mother are you?"

"Yours but I'll always support right and not wrong. The shit you're doing and tryna do is unnecessary and will get you in more trouble than a little." She walked back in the kitchen and left me there in my thoughts until my sister walked in looking bigger than a house.

WHAP! She smacked me so hard my face turned. I jumped up out my seat.

"What you gonna do?"

"Bitch, why the fuck you smack me?" I stood toe to toe with her.

"Why you go to mommy job acting stupid? Then, you texting Rhythm stupid shit about Sasha. She's knows how to take care of a child." I sucked my teeth. I did text Rhythm that my child better not come home with a scratch or bruise and I meant it. I'm not even shocked she mentioned it to Kalila.

"I can do what the fuck I want. That's my daughter."

"Not for long." She smirked and went to walk away. I don't know why but I grabbed her by the hair and swung her on the couch. I didn't give a fuck about her being pregnant. I was over people putting their hands on me and talking shit. I may not be a fighter but I was punching and smacking the hell outta her.

"Oh my God. Are you crazy?" My mom shouted. I could see her putting Sasha in the swing out the corner of my eye.

"I hate all of you. Fuck you and Rhythm." I punched Kalila in the eye and kept hitting until my mom pushed me off.

"She's pregnant Zahra." I wiped my lip because she busted it when she hit me in the mouth.

"Tuh! Not for long." I lifted my foot up and kicked her in the stomach and the chest.

"Ahhhhhhh." She screamed and grabbed my foot. I fell back hitting my head on the floor.

"What the hell is wrong with you Zahra?" My mother was so mad she drug me by the hair to the door and told me to get out.

"With pleasure." I stood, grabbed my daughter with all her stuff and left. Now all I have to do is leave town. Ain't no way in hell Jamaica will let me live after this.

I strapped my daughter in and rushed to the driver's side. I could hear sirens and figured my mother called an ambulance. I ran to the bank to grab some money and hauled ass outta town. I need to get away so Kruz is gonna have to get over seeing Sasha because we're leaving and never coming back.

"We have to take the baby out if there's gonna be any chance of survival." I nodded with massive tears falling down my face as the doctor recited those words to Jamaica.

"I'll pay you any amount of money you want, just do what you have to and save both of them." The doctor and nurse pushed me on a stretcher to the operating room with Jamaica holding my hand tight.

"I'm sorry Kenron. She was at my moms and..." The portable machine started beeping faster as I tried to tell him what happened. He shushed me with a kiss and continued walking on side of the stretcher. I could see how scared he was for me and the baby. I also peeped the anger he's desperately trying to hold in as well.

When I walked in my mothers and saw Zahra, I wanted to pounce on her for the things she putting our mom through. However; I remembered my baby and settled for a smack. Zahra knows she can't fuck with these hands on a bad day, therefore; I wasn't expecting her to hit me and she didn't. But once I felt the grip on my hair, I knew we were about to have it out. My fists were balled up and I turned to swing but she pushed me on the couch and jumped on top of me.

None of her hits hurt and honestly, I wasn't gonna hit her but she punched me in the eye. I started raining blows on her. My mom pulled us apart and this hateful bitch, lifted her foot and attempted to kick me in my stomach. I don't know if I were angrier about the fight, or the fact she tried to kill my child but I caught her foot just in time. She did try and kick me in the side but my hand blocked that one too.

Unfortunately, she connected with my chest and knocked the wind outta me, which is why I'm here. I couldn't breath and my stomach began to tighten. Once the pain kicked in, I knew something was wrong. My mother called 911 and here I am six and a half months pregnant having my baby delivered through C-section because of my selfish and hateful sister.

I was wrong for hitting her but she took it too far and me and my mother knew that's probably the last time we'd see her. Between Kruz and Jamaica, I'm not sure who wants to kill her more.

"Ms. Bell, you're going to feel pressure." I nodded and watched Jamaica looking at the doctor as I squeezed his hand. Twenty minutes later there was a release down below.

"It's a boy." The doctor yelled but there was no crying baby.

"Kenron, is he ok?" He turned and gave me the best smile he could.

"You ok?"

"I'm fine. Is he ok?"

"I'm going to the other room with him. I'll be back." He kissed my lips and flew outta here.

The doctor spoke to me about the things he was doing, as far as stitching me up. The nurse removed the sheet and lifted my bed up slowly. Another nurse pushed a different bed in and all of them took an end of the sheet to slide me on the clean bed.

The pain was bad and had the doctor not just given me medication, I would've been screaming for it. As much as I wanted to wait for Jamaica to return with good news my eyes closed and I drifted off into la la land.

****

"How you feeling?" Rhythm asked rubbing my hair towards the back.

"How's my son?" She smiled and showed me a picture on her phone. I slid my index finger over it. He had tubes in his nose, on his chest and bandages on his eyes. There was a light on him and the diaper was small as hell. I covered my mouth and cried my eyes out.

"My nephew is so handsome."

"Where's Kenron?" She sucked her teeth.

"What?"

"I asked if he could take me to see Kenron Jr. and he told me no. Talking about he needed to bond with him because you had him in your stomach all that time." She rolled her eyes.

"How did you get a picture?"

"That nigga took Kruz with him and he sent me a picture. Ain't that some shit?" I busted out laughing and then let the tears fall again.

"What's wrong?" She pressed the nurse button.

"I'm in pain and I'm so happy my son made it."

164

"Jamaica told us they rushed him out because of how early he is. He's gonna have to stay sis because he was only three pounds."

"As long as he's alive, I don't mind. I'll be up here everyday."

"You know I'm gonna try and kill her before the guys."

"Girl be quiet. You ain't no damn killer."

"Neither are you but when the time came, you did what needed to be done." She said above a whisper.

"You got a better chance asking if you can watch because those two are gonna search through high and hell water to find her."

"What happened?" I explained in detail and she was pissed.

"A smack is nothing and you were wrong but Zahra went overboard. She knew you were incapacitated too because she's never thought about hitting you. The shit was definitely done on purpose."

"I know."

"What was done on purpose?" Sabrina walked in with a bouquet of flowers and edible arrangements. Rhythm and I looked at her and busted out laughing.

"What?"

"Bitch, why you in sweats and a hoody that look like they your man's?" She put the stuff down as the nurse walked in asking if I were ok.

"Yes, can you help me wash up?" She told me she'd be right back.

"Listen. You heffas have become sisters to me and I'm not about to be arguing with y'all over your men staring at me."

"Girl, we know you not like that and men are gonna look regardless. We do appreciate you respecting it tho."

"Anyway. Where is he?" She glanced around the room and Rhythm started telling her what happened and showed pictures.

The nurse helped me out the bed and in the bathroom. Again, it was painful to move and use the bathroom but I had to be strong for my son. I came out and it was like a damn party. Jamaica, Kruz, Drew, a few other guys, my mother and even Rhythm's mom and stepfather came and brought Axel. I just started crying.

"You a'ight?" Jamaica ran over to me and walked with me in the hall. He found a chair and had me sit down.

"Yea. I'm happy he made it and everyone came to support us. I'm so sorry Jamaica. I should've known she'd do anything to hurt me."

"It's in the past ma and stop fighting her every time you see her." He wiped my eyes and kneeled down in front of me.

"My son looks just like me." I laughed.

"I wanna see him." He went to lift me up but I stopped him because the pain would be worse.

"Let me get the nurse to bring a wheelchair." He went in the room and told everyone we'd be back and went with me upstairs.

The nurse pushed me in and left us there. I had to place my hands in this hole just to touch him. I felt like he was being petted like an animal because I couldn't hold him. Jamaica must've known because he lifted my head and told me everything was going to be fine. I truly believed him but I wanted my son in my arms and had I not been in defense mode walking in my mothers, he'd still be in my stomach.

"I hate that she can get me to a point where my son almost died." My son grabbed my finger and I started crying again.

"It's in the past Kalila and he's gonna be fine. I have another doctor coming in tomorrow to check on him too." I smiled at how overprotective he is already.

"I don't know who's gonna find her first; me or Kruz but she's a dead woman walking."

"Is Kruz ok with it?" He gave me a weird look.

"What?"

"After Rhythm called, he dropped me off here and rushed to Zahra's house. For some reason he felt she would disappear."

"No, don't tell me that." I covered my mouth.

"She's gone Kalila and so is Sasha." Tears flooded my face because it's sorta my fault.

"Oh my God! If I didn't smack her she'd be here and Kruz would have my niece." He wiped my eyes.

"Don't blame yourself because whether it was you or Rhythm, Zahra was most likely looking for any reason to disappear because she knew Kruz was gonna kill her."

"Yea but…"

"Don't try and make sense of it. He doesn't blame you and neither does anyone else."

"I don't even know where she could've gone because no one in my family likes her."

"All you need to worry about now is getting better, making sure my son is well taken care of and you have a lot of making up to do when you heal." I sucked my teeth.

"No need to get mad. Just know I'ma tear it up so bad, you won't be able to walk for a while and even tho you'll be sore, those jaws better work." He winked and told me he'd be back after he used the bathroom. I better get ready for him because he can definitely have me walking funny and stuck in the bed after sex.

"Ok Ms. Mitchell, you are three and a half months. Would you like to see the baby?" The doctor asked and turned the screen to me.

"A'ight yo. Print the picture and take that dildo shit out her pussy." Kruz barked and I covered my face.

"Sir, this is how we..."

"I don't give a fuck. The only person sticking anything in my girl pussy is me. Now hurry the fuck up like I said."

TAP! TAP! TAP! TAP! The doctor rushed to do what he said and pulled the device out.

She told me to get dressed, handed me my prescription for the vitamins and said to grab my next appointment at the front desk. When she closed the door, I was fucking hysterical laughing.

"Tha fuck you laughing at?" He stood me up and lifted my clothes up like a kid.

"You are a damn fool."

"Why I gotta be all that?" Still on the stupid thing attached to the table, I wrapped my arms around his neck and kissed him.

"You can't come to no more appointments if you're gonna be acting up."

"I'm saying Rhythm. Why can't they put it on your stomach?"

"Babe, they need an accurate due date and they can't get one on my stomach. Kruz." I stepped down and grabbed my things.

"No one is putting anything in me besides you."

"Better not be."

"Were you this bad when she had Sasha in her belly?"

"Hell no because I could care less at that point about anyone being in her shit." He shrugged and gripped my arm.

"Did that nigga rape you in the motel when that shit happened?"

"I don't think so."

"How can you be sure?"

"I remember him pulling the gun out, hitting me in the head, jumping on top of me, me fighting him and then a punch to the face."

"Again. How can you be sure he didn't?"

"Kruz, the doctor would've told me and even though there was DNA under my nails, there would've been a sign. Are you ok?" I made him look at me.

"I was already pregnant before the attack happened but we can get a test if you want." I wasn't even upset if he wanted one because of what Zahra put him through.

"I don't want a test Rhythm. I'm asking because he raped his two nieces a week before the motel incident."

"Oh my God."

"I wanted to make sure in case you wanted to see someone or.-"

"Awww baby. Wait! Why didn't you ask me sooner?" I put my hands on my hips.

"I forgot and since you didn't mention it, I figured you didn't wanna speak on it. But seeing how happy you are, I don't want you to have a flashback and go into depression."

172

"Are you serious?" He leaned me against the wall and stared down at me.

"I know you think I'm ignorant and I am." I rolled my eyes.

"Rhythm I wanna be a part of our baby's life in every aspect. It means the mother has to be well taken care of too."

"Oh, you take very good care of mama." I slid my hands under his shirt and up his chest.

"Why you always tryna fuck?" My mouth fell open.

"That's how this one got here." He pointed to my stomach.

"No the hell you didn't."

"I'm just saying. You always want this dick, which means you're being selfish and not sharing. God don't like ugly.

"Sharing what? Ain't nobody getting this." I gripped his dick hard.

"Nigga, you see this." I lifted his shirt up and pointed to his tattoo.

"My name being there means I own this." I pressed hard and he grabbed my finger.

"And this one, means I own you." He used his finger to trace his name going across my heart.

The day he told me I had to trust him again, we went to the parlor and asked the tattoo guy to put my name in the box. To be honest, I was shocked because he always told me the spot was reserved for his wife. We aren't married so I had no idea he wanted me in there. What surprised me more, is getting one myself. He told me not to just because he did, but I wanted him to know I'm invested in the relationship too.

"Whatever." He opened the door and both of us walked out smiling.

"You riding with me forever Rhythm?" He asked and helped me in the truck.

"Do I have a choice?" He stood in between my legs.

"Not really." He pecked my lips.

"Why you ask?"

"Because we're about to go somewhere and I need to know you won't back out."

174

"We're we going?" He put my legs in the truck, closed the door and went on the other side.

"Remember you're riding." He smirked, picked his phone up and made a call. I paid him no mind as I sent the ultrasound photo to my mom, Ms. Bell and Kalila. I was excited to be pregnant again. The circumstances may have been crazy getting here but I'm still happy.

****

"Why are we here?" I looked at the city hall building.

"You riding right?"

"Ummmmm. Are you turning me in for beating Zahra ass?"

"Man, hell no." We stepped out and walked hand and hand inside.

"Hello, Mr. Garcia." Some older white guy shook his hand and led him inside. He opened a door to an office and some lady and other guy were standing there smiling.

"You ready?" Kruz asked with a nervous look on his face.

"Ugh, I guess. What am I ready for?"

"This." He reached in his pocket, got down on one knee and opened the box to showcase a humongous pear-shaped pink diamond.

"Oh my God! Oh my God! Oh my God! Kruz, what are you?" He lifted his hand and shushed me with his finger.

"Will you marry me?" My vision was blurry from the tears falling and the snot running down my nose had to be gross, but this man didn't move until I answered.

"Are you sure?"

"Positive." He smiled and like always, I melted.

"Yes baby yes." He placed the ring on my finger, wiped my face with his shirt and kissed me with so much passion, the guy had to clear his throat.

"Ok. Let's get this started."

"Wait!" He glanced down at his phone and told the guy to hold on. He returned a few minutes later with my mother, stepdad, my son, and my best friend was on FaceTime with Jamaica. They were with the baby and I appreciated the fact they did as much.

"Are we ready now?"

"Yup." The guy read off a few words and I asked if we could do our vows. I wasn't prepared but going off the top of my head, I had this. *I think.*

"Kruz, I never believed in love at first sight until I met you."

"Word?"

"Well it wasn't the first night because you were rude and aggressive but the night you came to me at the motel, I knew then. For you to go out your way to find me said a lot. The crazy thing is, I thought about you day and night afterwards and imagined what it would be like being your woman. Could you love me right? Could you handle a woman with a son? And could you stay faithful?" He put his head down and I lifted it up.

"You messed up babe but I think you're worth giving another try." I pecked his lips and continued.

"I often ask myself if this love is real and I know it is, by your touch, kiss, the way we are around one another and how you are with my son. I love everything about you and nothing or no one can tell me different. Kruz Auturo Garcia,

I'm gonna show you how a woman is supposed to love you more than I already have. I'm gonna make sure you know without a shadow of doubt that God made me just for you. I love you baby." I wiped the one tear that left his eye.

"Your turn." The guy looked at Kruz. He smiled, grabbed both of my hands and looked in my eyes.

"Rhythm, you came in my life at an awkward time and gave me a run for my money. After what I went through with my ex, I never thought I'd find a good woman. In my eyes, all women weren't shit but you showed me different and gave me a reason to fall in love again." When he said that tears flooded my eyes like crazy.

"Damn right she did." Kalila yelled through the phone.

"Oooh TiTi." Axel made everyone laugh.

"Rhythm, you intrigued the hell outta me and didn't take my shit no matter how dangerous I was. You didn't let me walk over you and trust me, I learned my lesson when we were apart and I don't wanna go through it again. It takes a strong woman to look past my infidelity and start over." I put my hand on the side of his face and pecked his lips.

"I did try my hardest to move on but no one could compare. Rhythm, I'm still gonna go outta my way to keep you happy and satisfied. I love the hell outta you ma and I'm gonna be the best husband for you, stepfather for Axel and dad for our new one." He used his hands to wipe my eyes.

"Well, I've never heard vows like this but I will say, good job." Everyone started laughing. He finished the ceremony and by the time we were done, Rhythm Mitchell was now, Rhythm Garcia.

"You really are riding with me?" We stood outside city hall with everyone else.

"I am but you could've at least let me wear a sweater dress or something."

"You look fine as always."

"But jeans tho? I know at my reception, I'm wearing two or three dresses to make up for this."

"You can wear whatever you want, as long as you don't show up naked."

"I thought you liked me naked."

"I do but it's for my eyes only." We started kissing until Axel broke us up by asking if we were moving into another house.

In all honesty, I loved the house we were in. Granted, Zahra stayed there first but after hearing the house wasn't made for her, I was ok with it. Besides, he changed everything inside, down to painting the walls. If you saw it now, you would've never known it had a different look and I appreciated it. I would've changed it anyway.

"How were you able to pull this off? I didn't sign any paperwork."

"Yes, you did." I turned to him in the truck. Everyone left and Axel went with to stay my mom until we came back.

"A few weeks ago, I fucked the hell outta you and mentioned some papers came in the mail that needed to be signed."

"Whatever."

"Anyway, I told you they were insurance ones but it was those and the marriage paperwork."

"You are sneaky."

"From here on out, always pay attention to things you sign no matter how good the dick is."

"Whatever Kruz."

"I'm serious. People mess up not reading the paperwork, which reminds me, we need to get you a passport when we come back." He pulled up to the runway that led to his jet.

"Where are we going now?"

"Don't worry about it. Just make this honeymoon worth it." We walked up the steps and once the door shut, I closed the curtain where the pilot sat, turned some music on and did a nasty strip tease for him. He tried to touch me a few times but I kept smacking his hands away. I could tell how mad he was getting and laughed.

"Let me fix that frown baby." I told him after stripping and the two of us christened the jet until we reached our destination.

I stood in the bay window overlooking the ocean as my new wife laid asleep. We were in Aruba on our honeymoon and had just finished making love about two hours ago. As tired as I was, my eyes wouldn't close due to the raging thoughts running rampant in my head, and the fact my daughter is still missing. She's not even six months old yet and her mother already acting stupid. Something told me I should've murked Zahra the night I showed her the tattoo with Rhythm's name in it but I let her live, which was a fatal mistake on my part.

Hell yea, I wanted her to hurt. I needed her to know what it's like to love someone and then feel so much pain she couldn't take it. People tend to ask how can I be a savage if I allowed my mother and Zahra to have what they consider control of me. No one controlled me, I didn't wanna be with my ex any longer and it's not like I was around her a lot.

Let's be clear; from gate my mother has always been big on raising a family with both parents and wrong as she may have been, I know she did it with good intentions. She only wants what was best for her grandkids and I understood but she fucked up thinking her ass was exempt from feeling my wrath. My ex on the other hand tried repeatedly to get me at her house and it never happened. I may have messed up at the doctor's office but that's it.

Being a savage doesn't mean I have to kill everyone in my sight. I do have the means to do it but it's not necessary all the time. The true definition of a savage is being cruel, fierce and untamed. I'm definitely all of those but I'm still human and my heart gets broke just like the next man.

Zahra was the love of my life regardless of the things that transpired in our relationship. However; I must not have been the same in hers. If I were how could she cheat, and with my brother at that? The thought of them two together still pisses me off. Like I told my mother, Kommon may not have known who she was, but Zahra definitely knew who he was.

"You ok?" I felt Rhythm's arm around my waist.

"I'm good. Why you up?"

"When my husband makes love to me all night, then gets outta bed, I have to check on him." Her head rested on my back. I turned around and lifted her face to mine.

"I got a lotta shit on my mind and Sasha is at the top of the list."

"You're gonna find her Kruz. Zahra doesn't have the means to stay away." I nodded, and carried her over to the bed.

"How did I get lucky with you?"

"I don't know but it damn sure wasn't off the first impression." I started laughing as she climbed on top and sat there.

"Sasha's room is so pretty babe." I smiled listening to her discuss my daughters' room. She decorated it when she moved in and hadn't quite finished but its complete now.

Rhythm loved Sasha as much as I because she still considered herself as the aunt. The only person hating on that, is Zahra.

In the beginning, it took me a couple of weeks to see my daughter because even after the results came in, I was extremely hurt that it could've been a possibility she wasn't mine. Then, I wanted desperately to murder Zahra but she was smart and began breastfeeding. I couldn't take her life because how would my child eat?

It wasn't until Rhythm and I were on speaking terms again and she told me, a mother can ween her child off the breast and there's even people who sell their milk. I definitely wasn't doing that but sure enough when I had Sasha, I took her to the pediatrician Axel goes to and asked tons of questions. The doctor said I should wait a little longer but time wasn't on my side because Zahra needed to die.

Anyway, I purchased the milk the pediatrician recommended and shockingly, Sasha took it with no problem. It's supposed to be like breast milk so I'm guessing it's why she did.

Long story short, the last time I saw Sasha was the day before Zahra sent her sister into early labor and that was over a month ago. Now with no leads, I still had a bounty on her head. The bitch is dead on sight and that's my word. I appreciated talking to my wife because she does try and make me see things from different angles, and sometimes the smallest conversations help.

"I love you Rhythm." I ran my hand through her thick hair when she laid on my chest.

"I love you too Kruz and we're gonna find her."

"I hope so." I blew my breath out.

"We will." She kissed my lips, moved down to my chest and gave me some of her A-1 head game. I went straight to sleep.

****

"Mr. Kruz, can we go to Gamestop?" Axel barged in the room just as Rhythm and I got dressed. We were on our way to see my brother. We came back from our honeymoon a week ago and you would still think we were there by the amount of sex we had.

I didn't wanna go to Kommon's because I really didn't wanna know anything that transpired between the two of them. However; she gave me some banging ass sex and I couldn't deny her afterwards.

"I'm going somewhere with mommy. Can I take you later?"

"Where you going? Mommy, can you make him go later?" She had him stand in front of her as she sat on the bed.

"Axel, what did I tell you about the game store?"

"We can only go once a month."

"Kruz took you last week and brought you three new games."

"Yea but..."

"But nothing. Kruz will talk you in three weeks."

"What about TiTi's boyfriend?"

"What about him?"

"He hasn't taken me this month and..." I chuckled because he was smart as hell.

"Once a month, is once a month Axel. It doesn't matter who takes you." He pouted and walked out the room.

"I would've taken him." I told her after he left the room. I'd never contradict anything she said in front of him. She came over to me.

"He has to learn that things aren't always gonna go his way. Besides, all he does is sit in the room playing the game."

"You not complaining about it when you be tryna fuck." She smacked me on the arm.

"Those are only quickies."

"Doesn't matter. It keeps him busy while you in here letting me blow your back out."

"Whatever." She put her sneakers on and went to get the door. Her mom was coming to babysit because Rhythm didn't want him anywhere near her house. Zahra may be hiding but she can't be trusted.

I walked down the steps and saw Kash laying on the couch. Him and Axel were watching some cartoon. Ms. Bell gave me a hug and promised if Zahra called or popped up she'd tell me. She was just as upset because of all the things her daughter did. I'm sure she knows her child won't be living much longer.

"Kash, don't leave from in front of Ms. Bell."

"Bro, ain't nobody tryna steal from you." He rolled his eyes and I looked at Rhythm.

188

"Maybe we should take Axel." I told her.

"Why? He can stay with his nana."

"What if Kash tries to steal him?" Rhythm laughed so hard she had to hold her stomach.

"I'm serious. That nigga will steal the cold air out the refrigerator if you let him."

"Kruz, stop playing me out." He walked over to me, and Rhythm moved him on side of her.

"That's what happens when you're a damn kleptomaniac. Don't nobody trust yo ass and you better not had ate none of my food."

"Let's go babe."

"Yea bro. Go with yo wife before we jump yo ass." He pretended to jump at me and I snatched his ass up. I lifted him off the ground by his shirt and laughed as his feet dangled.

"Mr. Kruz, I want you to do the same with me." I placed Kash back on his feet and lifted Axel up but in a different way.

"It's time babe." I put him down and told him we'd play later. As for Kash, I reminded that nigga what would happen if I even thought a spoon was missing. We got in the car and drove to the first stop, which I was dreading because I don't see this going well either.

****

"What's good pops?" We embraced one another and I introduced him to my wife. Rhythm didn't want me to have any animosity towards my parents for the bullshit Zahra did. She understood my take on the shit my mother was a part of but told me, she's the only mother I have and need to make amends, even if it's to let her know I don't hate her.

"Your wife? Nigga, I didn't get no invite."

"It was spur of the moment Mr. Garcia but I plan on having a huge reception and you're more than welcome to come."

"I better. What y'all doing over here?" He kissed Rhythm's hand and invited us in.

"Wow! This house is beautiful." She walked around the living room and stopped when my mother came in view.

"Kruz, when did you get here?" She ignored Rhythm's presence and it instantly pissed me off.

190

"My wife and I."

"Your wife? You got married?"

"Like I said, my wife and I just got here and if you want me to have any type of conversation with you, I suggest you acknowledge her."

"It's ok baby." I felt Rhythm squeeze my hand.

"Actually, it's not and regardless of the way she feels about my ex, she needs to respect any woman I bring here."

"What?" Rhythm snapped and me and my father laughed.

"I'm saying in general. You have my last name and about to birth my child. Ain't no other woman coming here."

"Better not." She let my hand go and asked my father if they could go on the porch to give us privacy. I could see my pops struggling because he knows how I get. I reassured him, I'm good. He walked slowly on the porch, kept the door open and the screen cracked. I could hear him and Rhythm discussing the pictures in the photo album she picked up on the way out. My mother continued standing there staring at me.

"I didn't know Kruz." I took a seat on the long sectional and put my elbows on my knees.

"How would you feel if uncle Shawn allowed some woman to come in his house to speak with pops and he never told you?" I referenced to her brother who didn't care for my mother either. It's not like she's a bad woman but her attitude and stubbornness kept my family away.

"Would you be ok with knowing another woman was in his face?" She put her head down.

"I understand Kommon is your son too, however; you should've asked questions or let me know and I'd ask. I mean let's be real. Kommon has never met her with me so at no point did you think it was odd for them to know one another?"

"I wasn't thinking."

"No, because you were dead set on tryna rekindle a flame I told you was burnt out."

"Kruz, I just wanted you to be a family like me and your father."

"I get it but shit don't always work out the way we plan. The minute I told you it was over and we can co-parent, as my mother you should've been ok with it."

"You're right and I'm sorry."

"Sorry can't fix a damn thing now and the sad part is, if my wife doesn't wanna fuck with you or allow you time with my kid, I won't say shit and you know why?"

"Kruz." She started to sit next to me and I gave her a look to stand where the fuck she was.

"Because even after all the shit Zahra has done, you still feel bad for her and it don't sit right with me."

"So, you're telling me there's no feelings for her?" The stare I gave must've scared her because she called my father inside. Him and Rhythm came rushing in and I hadn't moved from my spot.

"Baby, let's go." Rhythm took my hand in hers and stood in front of me.

"Whatever she said, it's not worth getting this angry." She leaned in and whispered in my ear.

"Let me make you feel better at home." She kissed my lips and had me stand with her. I swear God placed her in my life for a reason because I was ready to choke the fuck outta my mother.

"Is there anything else you need to say?" I asked to see if she'd apologize to Rhythm for the bullshit she pulled at the restaurant.

"Kruz, I don't like how this woman came in and has you speaking to me anyway you want. You were never like this." Rhythm placed her hand on my chest and asked me to wait by the door. I walked past my mother and gave her another stare to keep her fucking mouth shut and not disrespect my wife.

"Mr. Garcia, thank you for the hospitality and the funny stories about some of the pictures."

"Anytime Rhythm." He hugged her and she stepped in front of my mother.

"Mrs. Garcia, this is our second encounter and like I stated at the first one, if Kruz and I ever got together we'd have our mother to woman talk and there's no time like the present."

She moved the hair behind her ear and folded her arms across her chest.

"I understand the bond you had with his ex but she is his ex for a reason. Now if you don't want to deal with me, I have no problem with that but I do ask for you to stay away from my husband."

"Excuse me. He is my son and…"

"Is he? Because if I didn't know better, I'd say Zahra is the child you birthed by how hard you go for her."

"I just think they should be a family."

"Funny how you mention them being a family and you're tearing yours apart." Rhythm stepped back and over to me.

"My job is to keep my husband happy 24/7 and I plan on doing that but I can't if you're causing problems by tryna get him and his ex, together."

"Kruz you're gonna allow her to speak to me this way. Zahra would never…" Rhythm, ran over to her and was face to face.

"I'm not Zahra, Mrs. Garcia and because you don't know me, I suggest you stop tryna come for me."

"Is that a threat?"

"I only make promises and none have left my mouth; yet. But hear me clear."

"Let's go Rhythm."

"When Zahra is found, I'm gonna beat the breaks off her again and then take her life for taking my stepdaughter away from her father. So, if you speak to her, please let her know." All of us stared at her in shock. Rhythm ain't no killer but I'm happy to know she has my back.

"I recommend you get on the right team because if not, you're gonna lose this son too." She blew my mother a kiss and stormed out the house.

"Welp! I think my wife said it all." I turned and saw my pops standing there shaking his head.

"Pops, I'll see you later. Oh, and don't get Axel any games for three weeks because Rhythm said he can only go to the game store once a month." My father had been coming over a lot lately. He's the one who drops Kash off at the house if I don't have time to get him. He met Axel and that's been his partner ever since.

"Kruz." My mother tried to speak and I held my hand up.

"I came here to make amends but you can't get outta your own way to see that living the fantasy life of kids being raised in one household doesn't work for everyone. Rhythm is my wife now and she will be the family you desperately want me to have. It would be in your best interest to get on board with her if you want me to fuck with you again on any level. Peace." I walked out and to the truck where Rhythm was on the phone.

"Son, you did good and I'm proud of you." My pops came behind me. Rhythm hung the phone up.

"It's been a long time coming and I think she knows you won't come around if she doesn't change." He put his hand on my shoulder.

"We've given her a pass all these years for the way she's acted and it's about time all of us put our foot down."

"Yup. I hope she don't take it out on you." I helped Rhythm get in the truck.

"She won't. Your pops got what she needs." Rhythm busted out laughing where I turned my face up.

"Boy, you ain't never too old to fuck." He shrugged his shoulders and went in the house.

"That shit ain't funny." I barked and hopped in the truck.

"What he said is, but the rest isn't."

"Don't forget what you said you were gonna do if I didn't snap on her." I reminded her of doing something nice for me in the bedroom.

"Really Kruz?"

"Hell yea. I'm not with that telling me shit to make me happy. You have to do what you say and it can start with a strip tease because you do the damn thing." I kissed her hand and thought about the first night on our honeymoon when she gave me one. My dick was hard as fuck and she made me watch through the whole song, knowing how bad I wanted her. The shit was torture and she knew it but the after effects were worth it. We gonna have to meet up with Kommon another day

because my wife is about to put a big smile on my face.

"Mmmmm. You relaxed baby?" Sabrina rolled over after collapsing on the bed. We just went a few rounds in the bedroom and I must say, she's not only a stress reliever but a keeper.

The day my brother found out I slept with Zahra, I could see the hurt in his face before he swung off. I'm no match for him in the fighting area and even I were, I'd never hit him. I was wrong for sleeping with her and even though I didn't know until it was too late, I should've made it my business to inform him. As his brother it was my responsibility, and as his ex it was hers. Say what you want but my brother ain't nobody to fuck with.

I was happy Sabrina asked Rhythm to get him to talk to me because truth be told, I missed Kruz. I've been away a lot due to my job and I've wanted to have that brotherly bond but it was hard. When I came to town he wasn't around, vice versa and I did tell him to mind his business when he questioned mine. I wasn't being mean, I just knew he had a lot going on and didn't want him to worry about me. I'm the big brother and supposed to be the one looking out for him.

Anyway, Kruz whooped my ass so bad, I lost two teeth on the side of my mouth, I had some broken ribs, my nose was broken, both of my eyes were swollen and shut and I had to get a few stitches in the back of my head because I hit the ground hard. I think he went overboard but then again, anyone could tell he was hurt.

I didn't wake up for two days and when I did, I asked Sabrina how did she know where I was and she said Kalila told her. I had no idea they were close like that or she told them about us. She was heaven sent though I can tell you that. Sabrina nursed me back to health and cursed me out a few times along the way.

I was embarrassed like any man would be after getting his ass beat but she stuck around. She also told me it was my fault because I should've told him that day Zahra stalked me at the restaurant. I don't even know why Zahra was going through all that. She must've figured if she couldn't get one brother, why not have the other. I still remember when I found out the bitch was my brothers' girl.

"It's ok sweetie." I heard my mother saying when I walked in the house. I was home visiting for the weekend.

"Ma, who you talking to?" I stepped in the kitchen and got the surprise of my life, seeing Zahra sitting there. She looked disheveled and had massive tears running down her face. My first thought was, did this bitch come to my house to vent to my mother about us and how did she even know who my mother was?

"Kommon, when did you get here?" She stood to hug me and Zahra had a smirk on her face. My mother introduced us and it still hadn't dawned on me why she was here.

"This is Kruz's girlfriend." I dropped the water bottle out my hand and ran my hand over my head.

"They're going through some things but he loves her. And she's having your first niece or nephew." My words were now stuck in my throat listening to her tell me Zahra's pregnant.

I'm not sure if the child is mine but we did have a few

mishaps. Hell, the last time we fucked, I pulled out and noticed

the rubber was partially missing. I told her and she said it was

fine and that it'll come out when she goes to the bathroom.

There were a few other times it happened as well but I never

even considered her to get pregnant.

"I'll be right back." My mother left us alone and I

snapped.

"You're my brothers' girlfriend?" I had my hand

around her neck.

"Let me go Kommon." She scratched my hands and I

pulled away.

"You knew I had a man."

"Bitch, I didn't know it was my fucking brother and

now you're pregnant."

"It was a mistake Kommon."

"You're a fucking liar. We look alike so how the fuck

didn't you know and if you've been with him all this time, I

know you've seen the photos in this house and even at his. Did

you do this shit on purpose?" My mother kept pictures of us around the house all the time and so did Kruz. He's a family man and wanted to make sure his kids grew up knowing who their family members were, especially me since he claims I'm always away. This bitch had to have seen them in his place.

"Whose baby is that?" She sucked her teeth.

"His."

"You sure?"

"Yup." I paced the kitchen floor pissed off and thinking of ways to tell my brother. Its definitely not my fault but he's gonna be hurt and mad. He can kill her for all I care after doing this bullshit.

Did I have feelings for her? Absolutely! We were sleeping together for a year. Did I know she had a man? Yes, but like a woman waiting for her man to leave his wife, I did the same with her. She fed me all the I love you's, I'm gonna leave him and other shit.

I left her alone for a few months but once we ran into one another, it was back to us again. The crazy thing is she had no problem fucking with both of us. I wasn't any better but I had no idea it was my brother either.

"This is over. Don't call my phone, text or stop by my crib."

"Kommon, you don't mean that."

"Are you serious?" I looked her up and down.

"I still wanna be with you."

"I'm good on you." I went to leave when my mother came in asking if I wanted to talk to my brother and get him back with her. I could've smacked Zahra for the smirk on her face.

"I'll stop by when I come back to town." I gave my mother a hug and left. That was the last time I ever spoke to Zahra until I stopped by again and she was there crying again. I hated the fact she had been calling me and asked her to take a ride. She drove in her own car because I didn't want anyone seeing me with her. I pulled up at a park, got out, cursed her the fuck out and bounced. If I never had to see the bitch again I was cool with it.

"I'm good." I hugged her from behind and kissed the back of her neck.

"You tryna move in with me?" She turned over and ran her hand down my face.

"Kommon, you're never home and…"

"I planned on surprising you but since you brought it up." I reached over and pulled the drawer out in the nightstand, grabbed the papers and handed them to her. She sat up on the bed and pulled the covers over. I don't know why. She has a beautiful body and it's the exact reason that once we became a couple, I told her stripping was off limits. She wasn't a full time one yet but the Dexter guy had her and a few other women set up to do shows for the club. I couldn't have my woman showing off her goods, even if it wasn't fully naked.

"How did you do this?" She smiled going over the paperwork for my new office building. I made so much money over the years, I purchased a building to start my own insurance company.

"Believe it or not, I'm smart and its always been a dream of mine to own a business." She put the papers down.

"I know you're smart but I didn't know you were looking into this."

"I didn't wanna jinx anything, which is why I kept it quiet." She moved on my lap and stared down at me.

"I'll move in if you and your brother make it right."

"Sabrina, I can't make him wanna speak to me."

"No, but at least put forth the effort and if it goes nowhere at least you tried." I lifted myself on my elbows.

"Why do you care?"

"Because Rhythm, Kalila and I have become close and they have get togethers all the time and I wanna do the same."

"What do I get for it?" I lifted her up and slid her down on my dick.

"Whatever you want. Mmmmmm, Kommon." Her hands were on my chest as she started riding me.

"I'm supposed to meet him one of these days. Damn, you feel good." I gripped her ass and moved her in circles.

"Ok babe." We ended up sexing each other all day and I enjoyed every minute of it.

My phone rang when we stepped out the shower and I didn't wanna answer because it was my mother. She's been checking on me a lot and seem to appreciate Sabrina being here, but she has a way with words and pissed my girl off a few times.

For instance, she popped up one day and Sabrina was coming down the steps in only a t-shirt. My mom told her it wasn't appropriate to be in someone's house like that unless they were married. Another time, Sabrina was making me dinner and my mother told her to leave because no one needed to cook for me but her. Unfortunately for my mother, Sabrina let her have it in a nice way and my mother hasn't been by since and it's been peaceful to say the least.

****

"What is so important that you rushed me over here?" I stepped in the house with Sabrina. My mother wasn't in the living room and my father was on the couch staring at her.

"Pops, you wouldn't be able to keep up." Sabrina smacked me on the arm.

"Boy, you and Kruz keep underestimating my skills. You have no idea how good I lay this pipe on yo mama. Why you think she trying to make amends with y'all?"

"What the hell pops?"

208

"I'm just saying. I told her she better make it right with my boys or no more dick for her." Sabrina was hysterical laughing.

"Now Sabrina, if you ever need to see where he gets it from, my wife leaves after nine in the morning."

"I got you." He winked at her and the three of us sat in the living room cracking jokes until my mom walked in. When she laid eyes on my girl, she sucked her teeth.

"Remember what I said."

"I heard you last night Kommon." Sabrina put her head down and I had my mouth open because my pops really had her in check.

"I apologize Sabrina for the way I treated you over my son's house. It's never my intention to run the women off in my son's life. I just want what's best for them. One day you'll have kids and understand where I'm coming from."

"I appreciate the apology Mrs. Garcia, but I want you to know disrespect is never ok, regardless of how you claim to be over your boys." My mother nodded like she agreed.

"Also, I would never be caught up in my children's affairs to where I'm ruining the bond we have."

"Excuse me."

"I've been around your son for what has it been six or seven months right?" I nodded yes.

"And you've managed to disrespect me for no reason at all, tried to kick me outta his home that you pay no bills in and caused major problems between him and his brother." My mother tried to speak but Sabrina cut her off.

"You may not have been the force to disrupt their brotherly love but you played a part in it. Again, I understand the bond you have with your kids but this one right here is my business and I'm telling you now, woman to woman, you will not cause any problems in our relationship and if some reason I think you are, I won't have a problem cutting you off."

"Kommon." She looked at me and then my dad.

"No need to get them involved. We're having a grown-up conversation, right?" Sabrina smiled and I squeezed her hand. My mother didn't say a word. After a few minutes of silence, I asked again what she wanted.

"Kruz and his wife stopped by and…"

"Wife?" I was confused because I had no idea they had a wedding. Not like I expected to be invited but still.

"Yes, he went off and married her knowing Zahra is supposed to be the woman he gave his last name to."

"Didn't Zahra cheat on Kruz with Kommon?" Sabrina asked and my mother sucked her teeth.

"Wait! Didn't she disappear with his daughter, leaving him searching high and low for her?"

"Well yes but…"

"Mrs. Garcia, no disrespect but your priorities are messed up. I mean how are you even entertaining a nonexistent relationship with a woman who basically kidnapped your grandchild and betrayed both of your sons?"

"Yea ma. Why you want him with Zahra so bad? It's obvious he's happy because he made her his wife."

"I'm done talking about this because no one seems to understand what that child is going through."

"Bye pops." I grabbed Sabrina's hand and headed to the door.

"Bye Mr. Garcia." We walked out the house and got in the car.

"Zahra is holding something over your mothers head."

"Why you say that?" I pulled off and drove to the next spot.

"The only time someone goes hard for someone else is because they know something and don't want anyone else to. The question is, what?" I thought about what she said, and maybe she's right. From what Sabrina says, Rhythm is a good girl so if my mother isn't giving her a chance then something has to be up. When I speak to Kruz, I'll ask him.

"It's ok mama." I picked Sasha up off the ground and rocked her back and forth. I had her on the bed in the motel, and left her to make a bottle. I didn't think she'd roll off because she was asleep. She must've woken up and looked for me.

The first night I bounced with Sasha, I stayed at a hotel a few towns over and had no intentions of ever returning. Unfortunately, my bank account was depleted somehow. What am I saying, Kruz most likely had the shit emptied out to keep me from running away. Anyway, my funds were very low and the only place I could think of to stay was in a motel. The one in town was the cheapest around and I really had no choice.

I wasn't too upset about it because I bet Kruz had people looking for me outside of town. If they thought I left, it would make it easier for me to move around here because no one would be looking for me. The only thing I had to do is find someone to put the room in their name. I went through my phone and dialed the number of a guy I met a while ago.

213

His name was Teddy and I met him outside the club the same night Kruz supposedly first met Rhythm. I told him then, I was in a relationship but he was persistent in giving me his number. I never called and when I did, I wasn't sure he'd remember me. He didn't at first, but still decided to meet up with me. Once he saw me, he licked his lips and I knew his nasty ass would be down for whatever.

Funny how I've been in the same motel Rhythm worked at for the past two months and no one knew. I had Teddy get one of his boys to put it in his name and I've been here ever since. He's been giving me money to buy milk, diapers and other things I needed for Sasha, in return the two of us been fucking like rabbits. He was nowhere near as good as the Garcia brothers but it was decent enough to keep me satisfied.

If anyone is wondering if I knew Kommon and Kruz were brothers, absolutely. Shit, he had photos in his house and so did his parents. He wasn't around much, which made it easier for me to sleep with him.

The night in the bar, I didn't expect to run into him but being mad at Kruz, drunk, horny and curious as to what it would be like to experience two brothers, I took a chance. I had no idea the rendezvous would turn into a year of amazing sex between brothers. Of course, it was different but the thrill of it all, kept me doing it.

I could see how hurt Kruz was and if he let me move in, none of this would've happened. Kommon claimed I was the woman he wanted to marry but it had been three years before I met him and he hadn't even asked yet. Now he's with the Rhythm bitch, moved her in and now expecting. If he wanted the same with me, why did he take so long?

"Shit." I glanced at the knot forming on Sasha's head and became nervous. She's still a baby and any injury could be bad, especially; a head one. I called Teddy and asked if he could pick me up and take me to the hospital but he was outta town. I looked out the window to see if Rhythm's car was there and when I didn't see it, I rushed to call a cab and went straight to the ER.

"It's ok pretty girl." The doctor said when he came in. He asked what happened and I told him she was crawling and bumped her head on the table. If I told them she fell, I'd have to deal with social services and I'm not beat.

"We're going to do a cat scan to make sure nothing's wrong and keep her overnight for observation." The nurse put an IV in her arm and pushed some Tylenol through to alleviate pain. I made a call and waited for the person to arrive.

An hour went by and the doctor said everything was fine. She was placed on the pediatric floor and the room they had her in was quiet. There was another crib but no one occupied it. I sat it the chair and rested my head. Sasha had fallen asleep and I turned on the television. A few minutes later the door opened, closed and she stepped over to check on my daughter.

WHAP! She smacked fire from my ass and I jumped up.

"Why in the fuck did you disappear with my grandbaby?" She tossed her purse on the windowsill.

"He was gonna kill me and if he weren't, Jamaica is because of what happened to Kalila."

"You should've left Sasha."

"My daughter needs her mother."

"You sound stupid. How the hell are you gonna raise a child on the run?"

"As long as she's with me, she'll be fine. Kids grow up without their fathers all the time."

"Without mothers too. Do you know the position you put me in with Kruz?" I stood, grabbed my purse and asked her to sit there while I went out.

"Where are you going?" I asked for her keys and when she didn't give them to me, I snatched them out her hand.

"I have someplace to be." I stormed out and let the nurses know her grandmother is in the room with her.

****

"You have some nerve showing your face after the shit you pulled." Tania said when she opened the door.

"Move." I pushed past her and went to the mini bar she had for a drink.

217

"She deserved it."

"Kruz and Jamaica are still asking questions Zahra. I don't know why I did that shit for you?" She snatched the glass out my hand and stared in my face. She's the one who attempted to destroy Rhythm's credit for me.

See, Ramon is cool with Jamaica and Kruz because all of them went to school together. I think he graduated with Kommon but they're all acquainted. I met him a few times when I went to the bank with Kruz and he seemed like a down to earth person. Very nice and was about his business. Unbeknownst to him, I started asking questions to benefit myself. I asked when he worked and pretended to be interested in wanting a home loan.

I found out the information needed and told Tania, who I grew up with. She worked at the same bank but was doing mad crooked shit. When she told me all the stuff she could get away with, I paid her a hefty amount of money to fuck up Rhythm's credit. She didn't care because the money was good. She did that shit in minutes and even made it look like the transactions occurred in a different bank. To this day, they still don't know how it happened but they did put out a fraud case, which meant it didn't mess up anything. I was pissed when my mother told me that because the bitch didn't deserve anything.

She had a baby father with money who was actually in his life. Yet; she's running around with my baby daddy tryna wife him up. Doesn't the bitch know that I'm Zahra Bell and he ain't going nowhere? They better recognize this bitter ex or should I say they should've. I told them from the beginning how I'd be so I don't know why everyone acting all surprised.

"You did it because you're money hungry."

"Whatever. Why you here?" She had her arms folded across her chest like my presence was bothering her.

"Sasha fell off the bed and I had to rush her to the hospital."

"Bitch, why you here? You should be at the hospital with her."

"Because her grandmother is there."

"Kruz, is gonna have a fit." I rolled my eyes because she had no idea what was going on and I had no intentions on telling her. People may be aware we broke up but I still tell them we fucking and he stays at my house to save face. I'll be damned if I look like a fool for him.

"I'm about to go." She picked her stuff up and walked to the door. I poured another shot, drank, and left out with her.

"Zahra, they better not ever find out." Tania shouted at her car.

"They won't damn."

"Fuck you bitch. Don't bring your ass to my house anymore." I sat in the car and rested my head on the steering wheel. Those two shots had my head spinning that quick. I lifted my head and noticed a car ride by and followed it. If this is who I think it is, I wanna see where they're going.

RING! RING! The cell phone I took with the keys rang. I answered and instantly caught an attitude at what I saw in front of my eyes.

"WHAT?"

"Sasha won't stop crying."

"Give her a damn bottle." Why the hell she acting like she never took care of a damn baby?

"Zahra, she wants her mother."

"You're her grandmother. Do your fucking job and babysit."

"Who the hell you talking to?"

"You. Now don't call this phone again. I'll be there, when I get there."

"Zahra, come get this baby."

"Fuck that baby." I disconnected the call and continued following the car.

"Be careful babe." Rhythm kissed me on the way out the door.

"I will." I looked around the area and an eerie feeling washed over me. I'm not worried about Zahra tryna run up on her or Kalila because they can hold their own. This feeling felt more like someone else.

"Keep these doors locked and don't open them for anyone."

"I'm not."

"I mean it Rhythm." I hated leaving her at Ms. Bell's house but we were there when Jamaica called and mentioned Kandy's boyfriend was in the area. We had been looking for him too and this is the time to get his ass. But the feeling wasn't going away.

"Ok babe. Just hurry back." I kissed her, ran down the steps and hopped in my truck.

On the ride over, I noticed a car following me. Each turn I made, so did the person. I pulled over, waited for them to go by but they turned down a different street. If I had time to follow them I would. Whoever it is obviously didn't want me to see them and it's all good because if it's meant for us to run in to one another, we will.

I hit the block Jamaica was on, pulled up next to him and asked where he at. Unfortunately, dude bounced but Kandy was hiding in some hotel. Crazy part about this whole situation, is her father has been helping us find her. Evidently, he didn't care for her due to the shit she caused. If you asked me, I think it goes further than that. There's no way a man will be ok with anyone purposely tryna murder their child no matter how old they are.

"What's up with Geoffrey?"

"I can't even tell you. One minute he was at the place and the next, he's gone. It's obvious he has someone working with him again."

"Yea but who?" He ran his hand over his head.

"Hold on." He answered his phone and I could hear him yelling about something.

"Yo! We gotta go." Jamaica hopped in the car and had me rush to my parents' house.

"What's the rush?"

"Your pops called and said to get here quick. He's been tryna reach you but you ain't answering." I felt my phone vibrating a few times but I was worried about the feeling I had around Rhythm and with the person following me, I forgot to check it.

I jumped out when we pulled up and saw at least five cop cars. My father was sitting on the couch with Kash and a police officer. Others were standing around listening t the cop ask questions.

"What's wrong? Why the cops here?" I looked straight at Kash.

"Nigga, you better not had stole shit from nobody." He looked up with tears in his eyes. If he crying that ain't the reason because he don't cry for shit.

"Tha fuck is going on?"

"Kruz, they found your mother's car abandoned on the side of the road."

"Ok."

"It was set on fire and they think your mother was in it." I fell against the wall and leaned my head on it. My mother and I weren't seeing eye to eye but death isn't something I wished on her. Is this the feeling I had?

"Hello." I heard my father answer the house phone as a detective and more cops entered.

"Are you sure?" Everyone stopped speaking and waited for him to hang up.

"Get to the hospital Kruz."

"Why?" I instantly thought Rhythm or Axel was hurt and headed to the door.

"A baby was brought in with a head injury and they think it might be Sasha."

"Say what? I know you didn't just say a head injury."

"Hurry up son because if it is her this may be your chance to get her." He gave me a look that really meant for me to get Zahra.

The detective that walked in started telling me it's the reason he came over. The doctor called social services and reported the injury. They ran Sasha's information in the system and found out I'm her father, which brought them here.

"Call me as soon as you hear something about ma."

"I will."

"Kash you good?" He had tears falling down his face and I could tell he was hurting. He ran over and hugged me.

"You think mommy ok?"

"She's gonna be fine. You know she's to mean for anything to happen to her."

"Go get my niece and you know what to do with her mother." He wiped his eyes and backed away. I ran out the house with Jamaica on my heels.

I sped in and outta traffic tryna get to the hospital. It didn't matter how much I went over the speed limit or if I cop would pull me over. If my daughter was here, I had to get there before Zahra bounced with her again and I couldn't find her. We ran in the hospital and straight into Kommon.

"Tha fuck you doing here?" His girl turned around and that's when I realized she's the same chick who came to see Kalila in that tight ass outfit.

226

"I've been calling you." I couldn't say anything because I put his ass on block the minute I got bailed outta jail so it's possible.

"What you want?"

"Zahra called talking about I needed to get to the hospital because something happened to my niece."

"FUCK!" I ran over to the nurse's desk and asked what room Sasha was in. She told me and all of us ran to the elevator. If she had a room number it meant she's still here.

I felt my brother staring at me and could tell he wanted to say something. Thankfully, the elevator doors opened beforehand. I stepped off and noticed security at the door of a room and prayed it wasn't Sasha's. Unfortunately, I wasn't lucky so when the nurse pointed to the door, my heart dropped. The closer I got, the faster it started to beat.

"I can't go in." Security asked who we were and just as I went to step in, I felt someone fall into me.

"Oh my God, Kommon." Sabrina dropped to her knees as his body slid down. Blood was pouring outta his stomach.

"Oh shit." Jamaica yelled and pulled his gun out.

"Motherfucker did you just shoot my brother?"

"It's supposed to be you but y'all look so much alike, I fucked up. But this one won't miss." I smirked as Jamaica pulled back the trigger.

BOOM! BOOM! TATTTT! TATTTTT! Shots rang out and people were running everywhere.

"Where the hell are the shots coming from?" I pulled my brothers body inside the room they said Sasha was in, made sure Jamaica was good and closed the door.

"I couldn't see but I'm hit." Jamaica pulled his pant leg up and he had two bullets in his calf.

"How's Kommon?" I asked Sabrina who had her hands on his stomach tryna stop the bleeding.

"He's losing a lot of blood." I took my shirt off and put it on his wound. Jamaica was already using his belt to tie up his leg.

"Who the hell is shooting out there?" I turned around and couldn't believe my eyes. What the fuck is going on?

"Hey handsome." I kissed lil Kenron on his cheek. Jamaica and Kruz ran out so fast he didn't get a chance to drop her off at home and Kruz told me to stay here. It's not a problem because we're always here anyway.

"Mommy can I hold him?" Axel sat next to me and put his arms out. He loved Kenron Jr. and couldn't wait for me to have my baby.

"Daddy's having another baby too with Caroline."

"He is?"

"Yup."

"Wow. You're going to be a big brother to two babies and a big cousin to lil Kenron."

"I know and I'm gonna tell them what to do like a boss."

"What?"

"Kash bosses me around mommy. He says, because he's the oldest I have to do what he tells me." My radar went up quick because I'm whooping Kash ass myself if he got Axel stealing.

229

"What does he tell you to do?" I kept my hand under Kenron's head for support.

"He makes me get him snacks and juices out the kitchen. He said daddy Kruz doesn't let him eat at our house." I busted out laughing. I did like how close they became because Axel doesn't have any friends. He's always at one of his grandparents or at his fathers.

Kruz was definitely strict with Kash in the house and I thought about discussing it with him but I understand why he's that way. Besides him and his father, Kash pretty much got away with a lotta stuff.

The day Axel asked if he could call him daddy Kruz, I sat him down and told him to speak with his father. It's not like I had to ask but Axel's father is involved in his son's life and I wanted to make sure he's ok with it. Granted, my son can do it if he wants but both Kruz and I thought out of respect, the least he can do is let his father know.

Shockingly, his father didn't mind. Him and Kruz have yet to speak face to face but they've spoken on the phone plenty of times and exchanged phone numbers. I really had good people in my life and I thank God everyday for them.

"Daddy Kruz gives him a hard time but he loves him."

"I know. Mommy, he spit up. Yuk." He tried to push him off his lap.

"Axel you spit up on me all the time as a baby. My son can't do the same to you?" Kalila came down after taking a bath. It's the first one since she gave birth and I swear she was in there for almost an hour.

"No TiTi. I'm a kid." She ran after and tickled him until he had tears coming down his face.

I changed Kenron and asked her to grab a bottle. Axel went in the kitchen to eat a snack while Kalila and I sat in the living room watching the news.

"We're live at the scene where a gunman or men have opened fire on the pediatric floor of this hospital behind me. Officers are telling us they're not sure if it's a hostage situation but they've been told they're some fatalities." I turned the channel just as Axel came in and started playing with his

231

LEGO's on the floor. I hated those things. Anyone who has kids knows how bad it hurts to step on them.

"Who in the hell would shoot up a hospital and the pediatric floor at that?" She spoke low and I shook my head. It's very unfortunate that people will risk their life doing dumb shit.

DING DONG! The doorbell rang and we looked at each other. Axel had his earphones in thank God because he would've asked who it was.

I put Kenron in the swing and walked over to peek with Kalila. We may have learned our lesson at the hotel but we still nosy. The person had a baseball cap on with a coat and you couldn't see their face.

DING DONG! It rang again and the person turned around. It was Stacy from across the street.

"You think we should open it?"

"No." Kalila said and I agreed. We both went to sit and outta nowhere the front door opened.

"How you two heffas sitting here and didn't open the door?" Stacy bitched walking in with Kalila's mom.

"We just came downstairs. What's up?" She peeked out the window and all of us looked at her.

"CLOSE THE DOOR!" She yelled at Kalila, who was standing there about to do just that.

"Why are you yelling?" She hurried to shut it and I picked my phone up to text Kruz. Something ain't right if she's here and screaming for us to close the door.

"Y'all need to get outta here." I grabbed Axel and Kalila snatched Kenron up gently.

"What's going on?"

"Word on the street is your sister hired some guy to shoot this house up." Ms. Bell covered her mouth.

"But how? No one has heard from her."

"I don't know but it's supposed to happen tonight."

"All of a sudden, you heard loud music and then cars screeching outside.

"RUNNNNN!!!!!" Stacey yelled and all of us ran in the basement. There's a door down there that leads outside.

233

BOOM! You could hear what sounded like the door being kicked in. Axel started crying and asking for his father or daddy Kruz.

"THEY'RE IN THE BASEMENT. HURRY UP AND GET THEM."

"Oh my God. Run Kalila and Rhythm. Don't look back."

"Ma, let's go." Her and Stacy stayed back and told us not to stop running with the kids.

POW! POW! POW! POW! You heard gunshots and both of us stopped to turn around.

"I have to go back."

"Kalila we can't. We'll send the guys." Both of us had tears coming down our face as we tried ducking behind cars. We knocked on a few doors and no one answered.

A car flew past us and did a spin at the end of the street. When we saw it coming back in our direction we dipped behind a van. I covered Axel's mouth and Kalila rocked Kenron to keep him from crying.

"They out here because I just saw them." My heart was beating fast, pains were developing in my stomach as the voices and footsteps got closer.

"Take Axel and run the other way. I'll be a distraction." I told Kalila who's eyes were big as hell.

"Sounds like a plan to me." The man's voice said over my head. Once again, I'm saying a prayer to God hoping he spares my son and Kenron Jr.

To Be Continued…..